Nina Bawden

Nina Bawden was one of Britain's most distinguished and best-loved novelists for both adults and young people. Several of her novels for children – *Carrie's War*, a Phoenix Award winner in 1993; *The Peppermint Pig*, which won the Guardian Fiction Award; *The Runaway Summer*; and *Keeping Henry* – have become contemporary classics.

She wrote over forty novels, slightly more than half of which are for adults, an autobiography and a memoir describing her experiences during and following the Potters Bar rail crash in May 2002, which killed her husband, Austen Kark, and from which she emerged seriously injured – but fighting. She was shortlisted for the 1987 Man Booker Prize for *Circles of Deceit* and several of her books, like *Family Money* (1991), have been adapted for film or television. Many of her works have been translated into numerous languages.

Born in London in 1925, Nina studied Philosophy, Politics and Economics at Oxford University in the same year as Margaret Thatcher. Following Potter's Bar, she was movingly portrayed as a character in the David Hare play, *The Permanent Way*, about the privatization of the British railways. She received the prestigious S T Dupont Golden Pen Award for a lifetime's contribution to literature in 2004, and in 2010 *The Birds on the Trees* was shortlisted for the Lost Booker of 1970.

Nina Bawden

THE ODD FLAMINGO

B E L L

First published in 1954 by Collins

This edition published 2012 by Bello
an imprint of Pan Macmillan, a division of Macmillan Publishers Limited
Pan Macmillan, 20 New Wharf Road, London N1 9RR
Basingstoke and Oxford
Associated companies throughout the world

www.panmacmillan.com/imprints/bello
www.curtisbrown.co.uk

ISBN 978-1-4472-3595-8 EPUB
ISBN 978-1-4472-3593-4 POD

A CIP catalogue record for this book is available from the British Library.

Printed and bound by CPI Group (UK) Ltd, Croydon, CR0 4YY

Visit **www.panmacmillan.com** to read more about all our books
and to buy them. You will also find features, author interviews and
news of any author events, and you can sign up for e-newsletters
so that you're always first to hear about our new releases.

Foreword

When Nina Bawden published *The Odd Flamingo* in 1954 she at once became one of those writers whom other writers love to read. A very early crime novel of hers, this is a young woman's book. It displays all the vitality of imagination and language of the youthful writer, just beginning to be conscious of her own powers, and busily opening the box of invention to which she has the key.

One of the ways in which this verve shows itself is in the interesting cast of characters that soon walk on stage. Celia and Humphrey Stone, who are at the centre of the plot; Rose Blacker, Jasmine Castle (both these pretty young girls have flower names, it may be noted), and the less savoury Piers Stone and Jimmy Callaghan. The narrator is a young lawyer called Will Hunt, who is drawn into the tragedy by his friendship and love for Humphrey Stone.

We see the story through Will's eyes, he is the one who feels and lets us feel the impact of the terrible events that take place within the space of a few weeks. Will is a sensitive observer. As he describes the events as they hit him, they hit the reader too with force. Will speaks almost with a feminine voice. His tone is not masculine, although we are told he has loved a woman called Kate in the past and is deeply drawn to Rose. He is a romantic, possibly too dominated by his mother. Will Hunt is a lawyer, but shows little of the lawyer, in his speech and behaviour. He is at the feeling heart of the story around which all the terrible events cluster. Of all the people in it, he is the most sympathetic and the most destroyed. The author conveys this in a most touching and poignant set of scenes at the end of the book.

The main action takes place in a seedy part of London (since become notably smarter)—Little Venice. A shady club called The Odd Flamingo is where most of the characters meet and plot their own destruction. There are plenty of deaths: four, and one aborted pregnancy.

The Bohemian world it depicts is very much a sub-world of the 1950s. Unpleasing as it is, it would be very much nastier, tougher and more professional now. The customers of The Odd Flamingo take drugs and some of them are homosexual, but they are not in danger of AIDS. And the pregnancy of a young girl, which provides the starting point of the plot, would be less possible as a motive for murder in these days of better contraception and easy abortion.

The complicated plot is cleverly put together and the action is gripping; we are both surprised and shocked.

In this, as in other early books such as *The Lonely Child* (1956) Nina Bawden manifests the narrative skill, the sheer story telling quality which was to show itself in later novels, books for children, and work for TV.

GWENDOLINE BUTLER

Chapter One

The afternoon had been hot, without any breeze. The clouds were low and ominously grey so that people walking along the street carried umbrellas and mackintoshes and from time to time glanced uneasily upwards at the sky. The town, lying in the valley, trapped the heat and the day had been one of emptiness and exhaustion. I had been unable to work and yet not quite able to give up trying and go home.

Towards the evening thunder crawled faintly across the sky but the expected storm did not come. Instead, a wind got up and cleared the sky of cloud except for a fine tracery of milk-white stuff high up against the blue. So that by the time I had had dinner and changed my clothes and gone into the garden it was a rare, perfect evening. It was quiet, the shadows on the clipped lawn lay long and still and the air was heavy with the scent of roses. They had done exceptionally well that summer; now, in August, they were flowering as freely as they had done in June. Looking at the bushes I saw that the Crimson Glory had a light dusting of mildew on the leaves and wondered why I had not noticed it before. I was going to get the spray when I remembered about the nettles at the bottom of the kitchen garden.

I had been intending to clear them up for weeks; it was a kind of self-imposed fatigue. Just then there was nothing I wanted to do less, but I found the scythe and sharpened it and looked for my gloves. They weren't in their usual place in the shed and because I was too lazy to look for them I gathered the mown nettles with my bare hands until the palms blistered. I wrapped dock leaves round, my hands and cursed myself for my odd, urgent need to impose unpleasant duties on myself. I told myself that to do the jobs I disliked when I hired an adequate gardener could only be a pose on my part, a desire for the false satisfaction of a hair shirt.

But I was not convinced; as I put the scythe back in the shed I had a lurking sense of guilt. I wondered, idly, why I should feel this need to do something that I did not enjoy. I pottered slowly and happily round the rose beds, snipping off the dead blooms and thought about the guilty feeling.

When the telephone rang I took no notice of it for a while, hoping that whoever was calling would decide I was out; but the bell went on and on with a kind of monotonous impatience so that in the end I went to answer it with a blown, red rose in my hand.

I had no premonition of disaster. Later I remembered that there had been a bowl of roses on the table by the telephone and that, as I picked up the receiver, I had been comparing the dead bloom with the clear crimson of a bud from the same bush and wondering whether there was anything that could be done to stop the red roses from blue-ing so badly when they opened fully.

Celia said, "Will, is that you? Oh, thank God. Can you come down to the School?"

I asked her what was the matter and she said, "I can't tell you on the 'phone. Please come."

She sounded both frightened and distraught. It was unlike her.

I said, "All right. I'll come."

As I put the receiver down on its rest I knocked my other hand against the table edge and the petals dropped from the rose I held, scattering on the floor. I picked them up and put them in the waste-paper basket by the desk, thinking impatiently that by the time I got back from the town the light would be gone and it would be too late to do anything about the mildew. To-morrow would be no good either; I had to go to a bridge party. I hated bridge and I hated parties but I had always found it almost impossible to refuse invitations. It was one of the things for which I despised myself.

Backing the car out of the garage, I was irritated with Celia. I

2

hated to neglect my roses; they were my particular and cherished pride and I liked to look after them myself. They were not important, of course, if Celia was in real trouble, but I knew that what most people thought was urgent was rarely urgent at all. I told myself, wondering a little at my own resentment, that Celia had most probably forgotten to renew her driving licence and was in trouble with the police.

I reminded myself how much I had always disliked having friends among my clients, not because they didn't pay their bills but because it wasn't always so easy to charge them for a professional opinion when they asked for it at their own dinner parties. Even the nicest of people were always doing that and I could never understand why.

But as soon as I saw Celia I knew that there was something wrong that was more important than an out-of-date driving licence. She was waiting for me outside the School; as I drove down the hill I could see the pale blur of her face turned towards the car and when it stopped she ran to the door and jerked it open.

She was very white and her whole body was trembling. She was an attractive woman normally; she had a soft, reposeful look about her that suited her slightly faded fairness. Her features were too indefinite for beauty but she had a kind of gentle good looks that made more striking women look, beside her, a little ill-bred. Now, as she opened the car door she looked plain, almost haggard. Her eyes were wild with shock and her extreme thinness, which usually made her look delicate and younger than her age, now in a curious way emphasised it.

She said, "Thank God you've come, Will."

I said, "I came as quickly as I could." All my ill temper had gone; I felt only alarm at the sight of her.

She took my arm and led me through the gates of the School and across the green quad. The sun was shining on the warm stone and the air was very still. The doves were bubbling away up among the roofs and it was all very peaceful and out of this world.

Her hand was shaking. I could feel it through the stuff of my coat although it rested on my arm quite lightly.

She said, at last, her voice almost casual as though she were trying very hard to control it, "I don't know how serious this is, Will. A girl came to see me this evening, just before I rang you. She's indoors. I asked her to wait. She says she's going to have a baby."

I thought of the trouble they'd had the term before. I said, "But that's Humphrey's business. Anyway, not yours."

She sounded tired. "Yes, it's Humphrey's business. But mine too. She says it's Humphrey's baby."

We had stopped at the bottom of a flight of steps that led on to a terrace. A pair of big, rather ugly stone urns stood on either side of the lowest step. She was standing close to one of them, running her hand nervously over its swollen side, her head down-bent and still.

For a moment I felt nothing, and then the shock spread coldly through my body and I could feel the big artery in my neck throbbing fast as though I had been running.

I said, "I don't believe it."

I waited for her to tell me that it was a stupid, tasteless joke, knowing that it was not.

She said, "It's true, Will. I mean it's true that she's here and that she's told me this. Her name's Rose Blacker. She lives in the town. Her mother's a school teacher, I think. She says she's tried to see Humphrey and that he hasn't answered the letters she wrote to him. I don't think she's a bad girl, Will."

All the time she was smoothing her hand over the side of the urn in a gentle, abstracted way. Then she said, "I don't think she's just trying to make trouble. I think she's—desperate. She's got some letters that she says Humphrey wrote to her. She would have let me read them—I think she wanted me to. But I couldn't do it. So I said that I had to go and see to the children and I asked her to wait. Then I rang you up. I'm *sorry*, Will. This is almost as bad for you as it is for me. Almost as much of a shock, I mean."

I said again, "I don't believe it." I felt stupid and cold. Then I saw that Celia was watching me and that there was pity in her eyes. I felt, suddenly, ashamed that she should know how vulnerable

I was where Humphrey was concerned. As if it were a weakness in me.

We walked on, up the steps to the terrace, round the side of School House and on through the low arch that led to the little quad before the Headmaster's house. Before we went into the quad there was a low white gate with a notice on it saying "Private." We crossed the quad and went into the front hall of the house.

Celia said, in a whisper, "She's seen us. She's sitting at the window. When I came to meet you I went round the back way." She sounded panicky, as though it mattered that the girl had seen us. Then she said, "Humphrey won't be here for four days. It's the London conference. Shall we have to fetch him back, Will? He's staying with Piers. I can ring him up."

I said, "I don't know. I don't know how serious this is. What do you want me to do? Do you want me to talk to the girl?"

I felt empty and cold. The whole thing had the unreality of a bad play; I could not believe that there was a part in it for me.

She said, "Please see her, Will. Send her away if you can. I'm stupid and a coward but I can't talk to her just now."

She was playing with the string of pearls at her neck and they broke, suddenly, and rolled all over the floor of the hall. I went down on my knees and groped after them.

She said, on the edge of hysteria, "For God's sake, Will, leave them alone. They don't matter."

I got up and gave her the pearls I had collected. I thought she looked tired to death, ill almost, and I felt a sudden and violent pity for her. I wanted to say something that would comfort her, something to take the look of dread off her face, but everything I thought of sounded either platitudinous or merely silly. In the end I said, "D'you think there could be anything in what she says?"

As soon as I had said it I could have bitten off my tongue. To my surprise and inward alarm she answered me calmly and without indignation.

"I don't know, Will. There was a time, some months ago, when he was away quite a lot. Not often really, or for long. A night here and there and once a week-end. I was remembering about it when

I was waiting for you. He'd had some sort of explanation each time, I think, but it can't have been very convincing. Or I shouldn't have thought about it when the girl told me about the baby."

She looked miserable, and then she said, "You know, Will, if this thing is true, it may be my fault. I've not been the best sort of wife for Humphrey."

I was angry. I said, "Don't be a fool, Celia. You've done everything for him." That sounded false and tinny and I added, "You've always seemed so right for each other."

I meant it; that had been one of the nicest things about them.

She flushed darkly and looked angry, almost as though she didn't like to be contradicted. She said, "No one can possibly know." She ran her tongue over her lips and then she said unhappily, "I only meant that I'm not a very passionate person, Will. I haven't been right for him in that way."

There was nothing that I could say. I stared hard at the opposite wall feeling ridiculously embarrassed. Then I patted her arm and said heartily, "Don't be an old ass."

She sighed and leaned against me as if for comfort. We stood, for a moment, like two people on the stage. Her hair tickled my cheek. I kissed her on the top of her head and pushed her gently towards the stairs. I said, "I'll see the girl if you want me to. We can talk when she's gone."

She said, "Bless you, Will." Her face lightened and she smiled at me. She ran up the stairs and I waited until she was out of sight before I opened the drawing-room door.

A girl got up from the window seat as I went into the room. The evening light fell on her face and her appearance was so completely unexpected that for a moment I could only stare stupidly with a rising sense of astonishment and disbelief. I was not sure what I had anticipated; certainly not this.

She was so very, very young. I thought: a child, she should be still at school. She was small and slender and she held herself beautifully, like a dancer. Her face was pale and pretty; in spite of the mouth, tightened with alarm, it looked amazingly and softly innocent. She had remarkable eyes. They were thickly lashed and almost quite black, so very dark, anyway, that the difference between the pupil and the iris was barely perceptible. She was exquisite.

I stood, like a fool, and looked at her.

She said, "What are you doing here?" Her voice was gentle and pretty and faintly common. It shook a little as if she were afraid.

I told her my name and that I knew who she was. I said, "Mrs. Stone asked me to talk to you. She's rather upset."

Her mouth trembled a little and then she said with a kind of forced truculence, "To deal with me, don't you mean? She wants you to get rid of me, doesn't she? I know who you are. You're a lawyer. You can tell Mrs. Stone she can't scare me off like that."

She tossed her small head. She looked as proud as Lucifer but she was badly frightened. It showed in the way she stood, very straight and still with her arms pressed tightly against her sides.

I said gently, hating the thought of the things I had got to say to her, "There's no question of getting rid of you. I'm here because Mrs. Stone is an old friend of mine. You mustn't worry because I'm a solicitor. That doesn't come into it."

She said, "Oh, no?" but she sounded uncertain. Her skin was the skin of childhood still, soft and firm and unpuckered round the eyes. I thought that she wore no make-up.

I said, "Won't you sit down? It might help if we could talk about this."

She looked at me warily, her glance unexpectedly percipient. It made her look for the moment less young, but only in the way that a child will look suddenly un-innocent and old when it thinks of some special naughtiness.

Then she sat down obediently on the extreme edge of a chair. She was holding a large black handbag; she clutched it tightly to her as if it were a shield.

I sat down too and felt for my pipe, grateful for the business of filling the bowl and lighting up. I asked her if she minded my pipe but she stared blankly at me and did not answer. When it was alight I said unhappily, "This must be very distressing for you, Miss Blacker. Are you quite sure about the child?"

She said, "I'm going to have a baby and I know whose it is."

The words sounded as if she had rehearsed them. She looked away from me with a sudden, flouncing movement of her head which might have been embarrassment or deliberate rudeness, I could not tell which. Her face, in profile, was quite lovely. The nose was short and straight, the mouth and chin full and moulded with a childish roundness.

Looking at her, I felt a brute. I said, "Mrs. Stone says that her husband wrote you some letters. Have you got them with you?"

She nodded and I said, "I think you had better show them to me. You were going to let Mrs. Stone read them, weren't you?"

She opened the black bag and took out a fat envelope. She handed it to me silently; the astonishing eyes stared at me without any expression at all.

Inside the envelope there were six letters, each of them addressed in the handwriting that I knew too well to be able to think that someone else might have addressed them. I felt panic, knowing that up to this moment I had half-believed that the whole thing was a mistake, that Humphrey could have had nothing to do with this girl. Now I knew that I did not want to read the letters, that I would give anything not to have to read them.

The postmarks were clear. The first five letters were dated in January and early February, the sixth had been posted in July. I opened the earliest letter.

It began, "My own beloved," and it ended, "I adore you, Humphrey." It was a love letter of a kind that I had never written nor ever felt the desire to write. It was, in parts, lyrical, in parts unashamedly carnal. It was entirely tender and sincere. It was Humphrey's letter, not only because of the signature and the writing but because of the way the sentences were put together. It could not possibly have been a forgery.

When I had finished reading I felt that I had pried into something that was not for me to see. I read three more of the letters and they were as completely and utterly damning as the first had been. I felt both anger that Humphrey should have been such a fool as to have written the letters and also a kind of envy that he should have felt so deeply for any woman, in a way that I had never felt. I felt as dry as a stick and oddly old.

In the fourth letter Humphrey had quoted a seventeenth-century poet I had always found specially moving. "Thinke upon me as long as it is pleasant and convenient to you to doe so, and afterwards forget me ..."

I put the letters down in my lap and stared at the girl with a kind of wonder. There was a nervous brittle smile on her mouth and it made her look pert and a little vulgar. I felt suddenly and absurdly angry that she should have been so little moved by the letters that had been written to her that she should, so easily, have given them to a stranger to read. I told myself that in the circumstances I was being more than unjust, but the anger did not go.

She said, "There's another letter. The one he wrote after I'd told him about the baby." She might have been offering me a cake at a tea party.

I said, "How long have you known about the child?"

"About two months. I didn't tell him till I was sure."

"These letters. The first ones. They were all written about eight months ago. At the beginning of the year."

She said, with an expression that was completely innocent and without guile, "There wasn't any need for him to write letters after that."

The last letter was very short. Humphrey said that he would like to see her. He suggested that they should meet that week, on her afternoon off. There was no mention of the day on which she had her half-holiday; presumably they had met at that time before.

I put the letters back into the big envelope and gave them to her.

"Did you meet him?" I said.

She said, "I had to." She was twisting the dark stuff of her skirt between her fingers. She said that she had met Humphrey and they had had tea. Then they had driven out of the town and he had stopped the car in a lane. She had told him about the baby. He suggested that she went to see a man in London. He was safe, he said, a good doctor. He made her write down the address. The fee would be fifty pounds and she must take it with her.

I said fighting my own horror and disbelief, "Did you go to London?"

She burst into tears. She cried violently, her hands shielding her face. I got up from my chair and walked about the room wondering if she were going to have hysterics and if I ought to give her a drink. Then she stopped crying and looked up, shaking the cropped dark hair from her face. The tears had barely marked her cheeks but her eyes were shimmering with them.

She said, "I went to see the man like he said. I don't think he was a doctor at all. He had dirty hands. He told me to take my clothes off and lie on a couch. I said I wouldn't, not while he was there, and he laughed and went out of the room. I ran away before he came back. I couldn't stay. It would have been a mortal sin."

She spoke so quietly that I could barely hear what she said. Her head was turned away from me.

I said, "Did you tell Mr. Stone what had happened? And where did you get the money for this visit? Do you say that Mr. Stone gave it to you?"

She sat very still. She said, "He did give it to me. He gave me fifty pounds."

It was growing dark in the room and I turned on the light. In the harsh glare she looked tired and pale and young. She said, without anger, "He won't get away with it. He needn't think he will."

I said, "You know, it doesn't do any good, talking like that. It won't help either of you if this thing is made public."

"The baby's going to be public, isn't it? You mean it won't do him any good, don't you?"

She sounded slightly American as though she were seeing herself as a character in a Hollywood film.

"I quite understand how you must feel." The words I had said seemed to be totally empty of meaning. I went on, "But you haven't proved that the child is Mr. Stone's. It isn't as easy as all that."

She stared at me and then she said in a dead sort of voice, "Don't you believe me? I thought that if you read the letters you would believe me."

Her bewilderment was honest and pathetic and I felt a swine.

I said, "You don't understand me. I don't disbelieve you but I haven't heard what Mr. Stone has to say. Don't you see?" I hoped that I didn't sound as if I were pleading with her.

She did not speak for a moment. She looked wretched. She said, "What am I going to do? What will my mother say?"

I said, "Doesn't your mother know?"

She shook her head. "She isn't my real mother. She'll kill me when she knows. She's always expected me to turn out bad."

If the words had not been delivered so flatly I might have thought she was being consciously dramatic. But she seemed to mean them, to be without thought of their effect.

I said, with a kind of hollow briskness, "Come, come. You mustn't talk like that. Though I've no doubt your mother will be angry with you. It wouldn't be natural for her not to be. But I expect she'll help you when she's over the first shock."

She looked at me as if she didn't really see me. She seemed to shrink into herself. Her eyes were wide and bright and staring.

She said, "She adopted me. Gran brought me to Somer-hurst during the bombing. Then she died and Mother looked after me. She didn't want to but the neighbours would have talked if she hadn't. They all said how good she was to keep me and that I ought to be grateful to her. I am truly I am. But sometimes I think she really hates me. That's an awful thing to say, isn't it? And nobody guesses she's like that. They all think she's wonderful to have looked after me when my own mother didn't want to. That's what she tells everyone. That my own mother didn't want me. But it isn't true. She makes it all up."

She was shivering although the room was hot. Her eyes were big and blacker than ever with fear and her hands, in her lap, were shaking violently.

She said, "Please, you must believe me. I wouldn't have come if I hadn't had to." She put her hands to her face for perhaps half a minute and when she took them away her voice was steadier.

"I shan't be able to pay for the baby myself, shall I?" she said.

I said, "If Mr. Stone accepts responsibility for the child you won't have to worry about that."

There was a look of cupidity on her face. "He'd better. I've got his letters," she said.

She gave me a quick look and added hurriedly, "I shouldn't have said that, should I? But I'm so frightened. You've been ever so kind to me. I'm ever so grateful, really I am. But what's going to happen to me?"

There was fear in her voice and in her eyes, her words were a cry from the depths of the terror that held her. I wondered why she was so very frightened. I was almost sure that it wasn't entirely because of the baby. She turned her face away from me and I looked at the lovely line of her cheek and wished angrily that she seemed more of a slut. Less pitiable.

I said, speaking more harshly than I meant to because I was angry with myself, "There is nothing else we can do now. I'll talk to Mr. Stone and we'll get in touch with you."

She smiled her meaningless, bright smile. She said, "Thank you," like a polite child and got up from her chair. I opened the door for her and she went out. The front door was open and she crossed the hall and left the house without looking back. She went quickly across the quad. I could see her bright blouse against the dark stone of the archway and then she was gone.

I closed the hall door and went back into the drawing-room. I felt very tired. I wished I hadn't got to see Celia and talk to her. As she came running down the stairs and into the room I almost resented her.

Breathless, she said, "Will, is it all right? I've been with the children. They're awake. It's so difficult to get them to sleep these light evenings. Robin wanted you to go up and see his fish but I told him you were going home. What happened? What did she say? Is it all a mistake?"

I said, "Celia, I'm dead tired. Have you got a drink?"

It wasn't so much the drink I wanted as a respite in which I need not talk.

She said, instantly remorseful, "How stupid of me, Will. What would you like? We've got whisky but no soda. The children finished it this afternoon, so I know. I think there may be some gin, but not much."

I wanted to tell her not to chatter so. I said, "Whisky, please. I don't like soda. You get the whisky and I'll get the water."

She protested. She got out the bottle and two glasses and went to the kitchen for water. She poured out the drinks, putting in too much water so that the glasses were slopping over. She had always been rather clumsy and now, suddenly, it irritated me. Some of the whisky had spilled on to the carpet and I cleaned it up with my handkerchief.

She sat down in a chair with her thin legs curled beneath her. She looked anxious and unhappy and plain. She said, "Is it all right, Will?"

"No, of course it isn't." I wondered if I sounded snappish. "We shall have to hear what Humphrey has to say and find out a bit more about the girl. She comes from a respectable family. She's not out of the gutter. And she's not much more than a child. She's got some damaging evidence. Those letters that she told you about."

"They were really from Humphrey?" She sounded incredulous; she hadn't believed it. "Are you quite sure, Will? What were they about?"

I looked hard at my glass. "They were from Humphrey all right. There isn't any doubt. They were love letters."

She said, "Oh, God!" and the bright colour flooded her face and throat. Then she said, "If this thing has to come out will Humphrey lose his job?"

I said, "Yes, I'm afraid so." There was no point in saying anything else.

She said, without any expression in her voice, "You know a lot of people would like to see him go."

I said, quickly, "Nonsense," but I knew that it wasn't nonsense. I realised, with some surprise, that I had always known that Humphrey was unpopular with a great many people. I had never admitted it to myself before.

She said, "The governors don't like him. He's never tactful, he doesn't even try to be. Sometimes he's almost rude. He seems to enjoy making himself disliked—in that way he's like Piers. He behaved badly to old Purbright the other day. I know he's a funny old boy but he's important and he's very interested in the School. He came to tea and he talked about classics. It wasn't awfully interesting but he meant well. We haven't had a classical scholarship for years now—he was much too polite to mention it outright but you could tell he was wondering why. Humphrey got impatient with him and in the end he was downright rude. He said he thought we had all grown out of respecting dead empires that hadn't been able to keep themselves alive. It was a silly thing to say, worse than silly. The old man was upset but Humphrey went on baiting him for the fun of it and afterwards, when he got angry and went away, Humphrey said that it didn't matter. That he was a foolish old man and a bore. But Humphrey is foolish too. If anything happens Purbright won't stick up for him now and that's important. He'll need people to stick up for him."

Her eyes were angry and bright. I had never heard her criticise Humphrey before and it gave me an uneasy feeling.

I said, "If this thing comes out Humphrey will have to go anyway. And he's not been a bad Head. You know that."

She said violently, almost with malice, "You could never see any wrong in him, could you?"

I felt a sudden shame as though I had been detected in something ridiculous, and mixed with the shame there was anger against her for making my feeling for Humphrey sound so undiscriminating.

I said, feeling hurt and dignified, "I think I could, Celia."

She was swiftly contrite. "I'm sorry, Will. It was beastly of me." She apologised like a schoolgirl and she was genuinely sorry. She was entirely feminine and as changeable as spring weather.

My anger died. I said gently, "There isn't anything to be sorry about."

Then she said, "Will, couldn't we get hold of those letters? Pay her for them, or something?"

I was shocked, "Good God, of course not. What an immoral

thing to say!" As soon as I had spoken the indignation sounded slightly ridiculous.

She said, pettishly, "You mean illegal, don't you?" Then she looked as if she were hating herself and said, "Will everyone have to know?"

I told her. "We usually manage to arrange these things. It's only if the arrangement doesn't suit both parties that the thing goes to court. But even if that doesn't happen it'll probably get out. These things do."

She started to cry wearily. "Isn't it awful? I ought to be feeling sorry for her but I can't. I hate her and I hate Humphrey and I hate myself." She ended in a wail, like a child.

I could not bear to watch her cry. Not that I was in love with her any more but I had been, once, half in love with her and that left a kind of legacy. I got up from my chair and gave her my handkerchief. I said, "Dear, don't cry." I had forgotten that my handkerchief was soaked in whisky; she held it to her eyes and handed it back to me. She was almost laughing now and the tears were still running down her face.

She said, "How beastly. I shouldn't have let you use it as a floorcloth. Oh, Will, I'm so afraid of what Humphrey will say."

I said, "There's no need for you to be." But I knew what she meant. I was afraid myself.

She looked at me with pink-rimmed eyes. "You won't desert us, will you?"

I said, "This isn't my line of country. I can find you a much better man." That was true enough; this wasn't the kind of nastiness I usually dealt with and I wanted nothing to do with it. But I think I was a little surprised to find how strongly I felt about it.

She clutched at my hand with hot fingers and held it tightly. "Will, you must promise me."

I didn't want her to touch me; it was with a conscious effort that I did not pull my hand away. I said, "I can't promise anything." There was swift accusation in her eyes.

"You're sorry for her," she said. "I ought to have known you would be. You've always copied Humphrey, haven't you? Are you in love with her too?"

She was being unfair and absurd but all the same I felt treacherous and guilty, conscious that I had been, in some way, disloyal.

She said, with contempt, "You don't want to soil your hands, do you, Will? You never have, have you? Things like this don't happen to your kind of client. But Humphrey is your friend, Will. Have you condemned him already?"

I felt a fastidious fool. I said miserably, "Don't be an idiot. I'll look after the thing if you really want me to. I only meant that there are other people with more experience."

She let go my hand and relaxed in her chair. She smiled at me and I was resentful. She had persuaded me into a promise that I hadn't wanted to make just so that she could feel the burden of decision was no longer hers. I had always known that she was a dependent sort of person, but if I had ever thought about it at all I had always imagined that she would be able to stand on her own if it were ever necessary. Now, for the first time, I doubted that. I saw her as weak and I very nearly despised her.

She got up and drew the curtains across the deep window bay and the moment passed. I thought of it, afterwards, with astonished guilt. I told myself that it is impossible to dissect your friends and separate the good from the bad, that you accept them as they are, imperfect as they are.

When she left the window she was again Celia, whom I loved from long habit. There were bruised shadows under her eyes and her thin shoulders drooped. She had broken the strap of her sandal; somehow this made her seem very vulnerable and pathetic and I felt tender towards her.

I said, "Look, dear. I shall be in London to-morrow. I'll see Humphrey while I'm there."

She shone with gratitude and I felt very male and protective. I tried to comfort her further by making light of what had happened, knowing that she was easily persuaded into believing what she wanted to believe.

When I went I kissed her warmly and she looked at me with

great affection. She said, "Dear Will. What would I have done if you hadn't been here?"

I said, "You'd have managed. But you don't have to think about that."

And then she closed the door and shut out the light. I walked back to the car and drove home. I went to bed and for a long time lay uneasily awake.

Chapter Two

I woke in the early hours of the morning. It was hot and airless and I could not go to sleep again. I tried to read but that didn't help and I turned off the light and lay staring at the luminous switch of the bedside lamp.

I thought about the evening before and now, alone and in the dark, it seemed like a peculiarly grotesque nightmare. I thought of Humphrey and of Rose, of the people we knew and the shocked whispering over afternoon tea. I thought of all the paragraphs in the Sunday papers about respectable middle-aged men who seduced young girls. The palms of my hands were sweating.

In the end I got out of bed and went to the window. Below, in the dark town, the clock above the market cross struck three and the notes came up to me very sweet and clear. I gulped in the warm air and tried to think clearly. To-day I had to see Humphrey and I had to tell him that I knew about Rose. And that Celia knew. So far I was committed and for the moment it was quite enough. I tried to form sentences in my mind; just then it seemed agonisingly important that I should know exactly what I was going to say. It was the first time I had ever worried about what I was going to say to Humphrey and how I should say it. I had never thought of him before as I thought of him now, as a stranger.

I closed my eyes and I could see Humphrey's face in front of me quite clearly as if he were in the room. I found myself thinking, dispassionately, that it was a face that women had always found attractive. He wasn't handsome; with his big, beaked nose and narrow bones he was almost ugly, but it had never seemed to matter. Women had liked him; since he had left school his love affairs had been numerous and successful. Somehow, since he had married Celia I had assumed that he had been faithful to her. Perhaps it was natural for me to think like that; they had always seemed so happy and content together. And yet, remembering Humphrey as he had been at Oxford and afterwards when we had been in London together, it seemed an extraordinary assumption to have made. I began to wonder whether the life in Somerhurst which I found natural and easy might not have been, for Humphrey, very dull. It was a pleasant enough life if you didn't expect too much of it. I found myself thinking in a half-dazed way that it might be this that was the matter with me: I expected too little.

I found myself feeling resentful towards Humphrey and I began to wonder if I had always resented him and that it had, only now, come out in the open. When we had been at school together I had hero-worshipped him in a schoolboy fashion. He had been a year older than me but I had been clever for my age and we had been in the same form. That special feeling for him had ended before we left school and went to Oxford together but I had never felt about anyone else in quite the same way.

He was sure of himself, volatile and never gloomy. Life with him had been amusing and always unexpected. He was a good person to be with and he never made you feel a passenger. He was charming, witty and mercurial. I suppose it was because I felt myself to be none of these things that I had always felt for him, besides affection, a kind of admiration that was coloured by my boyhood feeling for him and almost entirely uncritical. It was not, as Celia said, that I could see no wrong in him; rather that I had not looked for it. He had been, for me, a quite special person whom I did not judge.

He got easily the things that I had to work hard for; amusements and friends and money. I told myself that this probably explained my present anger, that it is hard not to be angry with people who, having got a great deal in life, make a mess of it.

I looked at my watch and saw that it was nearly four o'clock. I was cramped and cold. I knew that it would be sensible, knowing that I was not going to be able to sleep, to get up and dress. Instead

I went back to bed and lay waiting for the next hour to strike. I must have slept then, if only momentarily, because the next time I looked at the window it was light with the dawn.

I got up and dressed slowly to fill in the time and went to the kitchen to make coffee. My eyes were sticky with exhaustion and when I had drunk the coffee I felt worse instead of better.

I wrote a note for the charwoman and went to the station to catch the early train. I usually drove to town but my head was heavy and dull and I felt that I could not face the long, traffic-blocked crawl from the suburbs to the city.

It was too early for the business men at the station and the platform was deserted. When the train came in it was almost empty. I found a carriage to myself and slept all the way to London, waking up with a bad taste in my mouth. I bought a paper on the station and went to the buffet for breakfast. The waitress was yawning and the place smelt of grease and cabbage. I ate scrambled eggs and stared at the paper without reading it.

It was not too early now to ring the flat. I paid the bill and went to the telephone booths. The station was busy and they were full. I felt relieved; there was time, before my first business appointment, to go to the flat and see Humphrey. It might be easier to see him and it would put off a bad moment.

I started down the slope to the tube trains and then, seized by an odd sense of urgency, I turned back and went to the taxi rank. I gave the address to the driver and got into the cab, leaning back against the cushions with a sick feeling in my stomach. I was having a bad attack of cowardice and I despised myself for it.

The taxi went down unfamiliar back streets past houses and village-like groups of shops where tired women with curlers in their hair walked with baskets and prams. We came out of the back streets into the known tumult of Marble Arch and drove up the Edgware Road, past the cinemas and the pawn shops and the dingy jewellers, up the rise and down into Maida Vale. We turned to the left and stopped outside the flat.

I paid the driver and went up the steps, through the open door with the stained glass fanlight and up the dark stairs. I stopped at the door of the first floor flat and rang the bell. The door was opened by a woman with a flat, muddy face.

I said, "I want to see Mr. Stone. Mr. Humphrey Stone."

"Yes," said the woman. She moved away from the door and I stepped into the tiny hallway. The flat was stiflingly hot; Piers kept the central heating on throughout the year.

A voice called through an open doorway and, reluctantly, because above all things I had hoped to avoid Piers, I went into the room.

He was sitting up in bed, his fat shoulders covered with purple silk pyjamas, leaning back against the white pillows. He looked opulent; a breakfast tray was balanced on his knees and the morning papers lay on a table beside the bed. The skin of his face was as scrubbed and rosy and clean as a schoolboy's straight from the bath; he looked more like a decadent Roman than ever. The Siamese cat crouched by his hand; when I came in it put back its ears and lifted the snake-like head with the pale, crooked eyes.

Piers said, "Well. William the Good. I'm delighted to see you, dear boy." He called everyone "dear boy" with the slightest inflection of contempt in the voice that was a little too urbane, a little too public school. His bright little eyes sparkled with malice and I tried not to look at him. I hated to see how like Humphrey he was, as though he were Humphrey grown old and soggy and fat. They had the same sharp-ridged nose, the same thin, curving mouth.

I said, "I want to see Humphrey. Is he still in bed?"

Piers chuckled. "Of course not, dear boy. I didn't think you'd come to see me, you know. Humphrey's not in bed; he's at his conference of pedagogues. He won't be back till late to-night but I can tell you where to find him. Is it important. Is everything all right?"

His eyes were greedy and curious. I said, "I should like to see him, that's all. There's nothing wrong."

I thought that Piers looked disappointed. "He said he might go to a club in the Fulham Road after dinner. A nasty little place. But then Humphrey has always had a *nostalgie de la boite.*" He smiled with sudden, spiteful enjoyment. "You know he doesn't get enough *boue* in Somerhurst with that nice virgin he's married to. Does she know that, I wonder? Dear Celia, she does dislike me so. Now what is the name of that club?"

He frowned, pretending to think, all the time watching me slyly, with pleasure. I waited and said nothing, not wanting to let him see that he had made me angry and uncomfortable; it was what he wanted. I had found that out long ago.

Once I had stayed in the flat with Humphrey for part of the long vacation. It had been apparent, from the beginning, that Piers had not wanted me there. I had not understood why. I had, I think, been young for my age, I know I had been clumsy and shy. I had been an easy target for Piers's brand of contemptuous wit.

I had tried hard; I had learned to laugh at obscenities that privately shocked me because I knew that they were intended to shock me. I had tried to adopt an easy, man-of-the-world attitude. Naturally a Puritan, I had endeavoured to pretend that I was not.

Of course I had not succeeded. Piers was too clever and too venomous and my own defences too fragile. In the end, as had been inevitable, I had lost my temper and told Piers, in an outburst of trembling invective, what I thought of him.

He had listened to me in chilly silence and when I had stumbled to the end he had said a number of brutal things. Among them, that I was a middle-class prig whose life would never be anything but excessively dull, that I was crass, stupid and not at all amusing. There had been a lot more of it besides, all of it near enough to the truth to be wounding. Until that moment I had not realised the extent of Piers's hatred for me; when he had finished I knew all about the hatred but I did not understand it. I had felt shamed and dirty and oddly afraid.

Piers said, "I have it now. The Odd Flamingo. Dreadful place with coarse paintings all over the walls. You'll probably enjoy it. Provincials do. They think it is Bohemia. Will you have coffee?"

I said, "No thank you. I have to meet a client at eleven."

Piers smiled, without friendliness. "Busy, aren't you, dear boy? Work is one of the things I have never been able to fit in. Life's too short. Why work, anyway, when so much is there for the taking? I work in my own way, of course. Aggie wakes me when

22

she comes in and brings me my breakfast and I sit, propped up on the pillows like an elderly tart"—he liked the phrase and repeated it—"like an elderly tart, and watch the form. Hard work, racing, you know." He added piously, "I thank God that with racing and women my life has been pleasantly supplied."

He settled back against the pillows and began to pour his coffee. He tucked a spotless napkin under his chin. I noticed his hands; they were beautifully shaped, well-cared for and fastidiously clean. I wondered if he shaved the hair off the backs of them and decided that he did; there were dark bristles in the smoothness of the skin. For some reason this gave me a feeling of faint disgust.

Out in the street the air of the summer morning was clean and fresh after the staleness of the flat. I took a train to the city and almost forgot to get out at the Bank because I was wondering why Humphrey should still be going to The Odd Flamingo. That the place should be still in existence surprised me; it was fifteen years since I had first heard of it. We had just come down from Oxford and it had seemed, then, a rather dashing little place to belong to. It had been frequented by small criminals and down-at-heel prostitutes and we had felt that we were seeing life. Later, when the squalor and the general seediness of the place became apparent, I had allowed my membership to lapse. It had never occurred to me that Humphrey had not done likewise.

The day was hot and long and the things I had to do seemed very dull. I had dinner at my club; there was no one there that I knew and I was glad of it. I drank more than I usually did and tried to forget the distaste I felt for the job I had to do. I told myself that I must be detached about it, that I must forget that Humphrey was my friend and that I had always thought him a rather special sort of person. Until the thing was sorted out I must think of him as a client who had got himself into a mess. I would have to tell him that we should have to offer the girl maintenance for the child unless she could be persuaded to offer it for adoption. If she turned nasty and applied to the justices for a summons she wouldn't be awarded more than twenty shillings a week. We could do better than that. With luck we might keep the whole thing quiet.

I paid my bill and caught a bus to Chelsea. It was nearly nine o'clock. The window displays were lighting up and the evening sky threw a blue twilight over the streets. I got off the 'bus at the stop I remembered and walked, looking for the club. When I came to the dingy door the name was painted over a lighted fanlight at the top.

Inside the door, the stairs leading to the basement were immediately in front of me; to the side was a narrow, lighted box tenanted by a dark, angry-looking man. He looked up and said, "Got your card?"

He looked a foreigner but he spoke with the accent of Bermondsey.

I said, "I haven't got a card. I'm looking for a friend. A Mr. Stone. He's a member, I think."

"You'll have to join if you want to go in," the man said. He eyed me implacably, with dislike.

I said helplessly, "All right then. What do I do?"

He pushed a dirty yellow form at me. "Sign one of these," he said. "It's ten shillings for six months."

The form said that The Odd Flamingo was licenced to serve drinks from three p.m. to twelve midnight. I signed the form, pushed a note through the grill, and went down the uninviting stairs. At the bottom there was a door leading to a lavatory; it swung open on drooping hinges disclosing a cracked washbasin and another door beyond. There was no door into the club; a curtain hung across the opening where the door had been. I pushed the curtain aside and beyond it there was a long, narrow room with apparently no ventilation so that the heat inside was solid, like a wall. At the nearer end of the room a bar had been built along one wall and there were a few, shabby chairs and plastic-topped tables painted in bright, chipped colours. The other half of the room was used as a dance floor; on a raised patform at the end three dispirited-looking men were playing a jazz tune. They played softly, not quite on the beat, as though they knew that no one would dance.

It was all much as I remembered it; the only thing that seemed to be new was the decoration on the walls of the club. They had

24

been covered with painted, bright flamingos with thin, pink legs and feathered bodies but in each case instead of the long neck there was the upper part of a girl's body drawn with sharp, bare breasts and a flat, smiling face. The drawings had been done with skill and wit; they were intended to excite and amuse but they did neither. They gave me a bad taste in the mouth.

The people were the same kind of people. There was the usual mixture of lesbians and pimps with a sprinkling of students who had come to see the fun. Most of them looked bored.

I leaned against the bar and watched the doorway. After a little I felt too conspicuously alone and went to a table against the opposite wall. The club filled up slowly and noisily with grey-haired women in mannish coats and pretty boys with lipstick on their mouths. At about ten o'clock Humphrey came in. He had a girl with him, a tall girl with a long, clever face.

She had changed very little in ten years. Astonishingly, I felt my pulses quicken slightly and I felt a fool. I half-hoped they would not see me.

But they did. Humphrey smiled at the girl briefly and politely and then his eyes searched the club as though he were looking for someone else. He looked distinguished and a little rakish, his pale hair shone silkily under the light. He saw me and came across the room through the close-packed tables.

"Will," he said, "how very nice. Seeking me out in my low haunts, you dog."

His voice was forced and over-jocular as if he were embarrassed at finding me there. The girl had followed him uncertainly.

He said, "Will, this is Kate."

She recognised me all right. She smiled and held out her hand and said, "You've introduced us a little late." Her voice was natural and composed; it seemed that she felt no awkwardness at all.

Humphrey said, "Back in a minute," and made his way towards the bar. Kate stood by the table and grinned at me.

"How *are* you, Willy? You do know who I am, don't you?" She was the only person who had ever called me Willy.

I said, "Of course I know you, Kate. I didn't know that you

knew Humphrey." As far as I remembered, they had never met; at the time that I had been in love with her I had been alone in London.

She said, "I don't. I picked him up outside. He dropped his card on the pavement and I helped him look for it. He's tight."

She smiled at me in the way I remembered. She said,

"Do you want to talk to your Humphrey? I won't stay if you do."

I shook my head a moment too late. She said, "There are some people that I know over there." She jerked her head in the direction of the dance floor. She turned to go and then she stopped a moment and said in a voice that was wholly serious, "It's nice to see you again, Willy dear."

She sounded as though she meant it and she left me shaken by an almost forgotten emotion so that when Humphrey came back with the drinks I did not notice him until he said,

"Penny for them, Will? Where's the girl? You'd better have her drink."

He put a whisky in front of me and drank his own quickly, as if he had needed it. His movements were quick and nervous, his grey eyes unnaturally clear and bright. When he spoke the vowels were slurred a little as though he had been drinking a good deal.

He said, "D'you know that girl? Not your type at all, Will. Nasty little bit of goods, I shouldn't wonder."

I didn't want to talk to him about Kate. I said, as casually as I could, "I knew her once. Do you?"

He frowned. "I don't think so. The face is familiar. I suppose I must have seen her about. I picked her up outside." Then he gave me a sober look. "Everything all right, Will? Nothing wrong at home?"

My mouth was dry. I said, "There is something. A girl. Her name's Rose Blacker." I gulped at my drink and finished it. "She went to see Celia last night. Celia rang me up and asked me to go down to the School."

I had been prepared for surprise and perhaps indignation. He did, in fact, go white and the lines round his mouth tightened angrily but it did not seem, somehow, that he was more than annoyed. Indeed, after a moment, his face relaxed and he looked almost relieved as though he had been expecting something worse. I did not understand why he should look like this; at first I thought that he was taking the news too lightly and it angered me. He said, "Damn her. Why did she have to do that? What good did she think it would do?"

I said coldly, "Don't you know why she went? She's going to have your child. She went to see Celia because she couldn't see you."

He said, "My child? And you believed her, Will?"

I said, "It was difficult not to believe her. She had some letters you had written to her."

That went home. He said, "She gave them to you to read?" He put his hands across his eyes; his anger and humiliation were almost tangible. He said, "We can't talk in here. Let's get out of it."

He got up abruptly and pushed his way through the room which was crowded now, to the doorway. He left a book and some papers behind on the table. I picked them up and followed him.

I passed by the table where Kate was sitting next to a little, drunken man who clutched at her arm with tiny fingers. He was saying, "You remind me of a great, big, beautiful lioness." His mouth was wet, his eyes narrow and bright. Kate looked up at me with comic despair.

She said, "He's a soak, Willy. Like to take him with you?" I thought she was unhappy in spite of the smile. I wanted to ask her where she was living and if I could see her, but I didn't. I think I was afraid that she would laugh at me and I wasn't sure that I wanted to see her badly enough to risk that.

Humphrey was in the street; I had been half-afraid that he would not wait. He was pacing up and down. In the dusk he looked very young, his flaxen hair tumbled over his forehead. When I joined him he started to walk very fast, his limp very noticeable, his eagle nose enormous against the lamplight.

After a bit, he said, "I've been a fool, Will. A perfect bloody fool."

I didn't say anything. I didn't know what to say. Perhaps if I had tried to find the right words he might have told me then, more than he did tell me. Although it might not have helped him or altered anything.

He said, "Did you believe her, Will? When she told you about the child?"

I told him that I didn't know. I could not say to him that I had believed her, that there had been no doubt in my mind.

He swore softly and savagely. Then he said, "If you, of all people, believed her, then there isn't any hope for me."

At the time I thought he was being dramatic. I said, impatiently, "Is it your child?" knowing that I was afraid of what he might answer.

He shook his head. "It can't be. I don't know whose it is but it isn't mine."

I said, "The letters? I didn't want to read them, you know, but I had to know what proof she had."

He stood still and the light from the street lamp fell on his pale and narrow face. He said, "I was in love with her when I wrote those letters. Maybe I still am. Anyway, I was then. I may be a swine and a middle-aged fool but I loved her. For a little while there wasn't anyone who was so completely real to me. I don't think I expected her to understand how I felt about her or that I minded very much because she didn't. I meant those letters, Will."

He started to walk again so quickly that I could barely keep up with him. Then he stopped and swivelled round to face me. He said, "But she isn't going to have my child. I swear it, Will."

I said, "When did she tell you about it?"

"About a month ago. Earlier, perhaps. She wrote to me and we met. She said she was in trouble and the man had refused to help her. She didn't say who he was and I didn't ask. I gave her fifty pounds. Then she wrote again and I didn't answer her letters. How could I?"

I thought of what Rose had told me about the fifty pounds. I couldn't tell Humphrey about that. Not yet.

I said, "If she applies for an order against you she'll get it on the strength of those letters. There's no sure way of getting at the truth in these things."

Humphrey said, "You don't believe me, then." It was a statement, not a question. He sounded both incredulous and resentful, two emotions so natural in the circumstances that I felt a little gentler towards him. I wished that we had not been so honest with each other always—although it was beginning to appear that the honesty had been mostly on my side—so that now it would be easier to lie.

He said, with a sudden outburst of anger, "I don't know why I care about your bloody self-righteous opinion, but I do. I don't know why this thing happened. I should have thought about a hell of a lot of things I didn't think about. I'd never been unfaithful to Celia before, you know. Piers thinks that's damn funny. I'm not sure that I don't agree with him. Anyway, there you have it. For a little while she was the most precious thing in my life and in the end I put a stop to it. I'm not sure, now, that I know why. Maybe I was just scared because she'd come to mean so much to me. I didn't see her again until after she'd written and told me she was pregnant. I was sorry for her, then. I wanted to help her. I didn't think she would do anything like this. It's a kind of blackmail, isn't it?"

He stopped short and seemed, suddenly, confused as though he had intended to say something else and decided against it. Then he said in an astonished voice, "It's so unlikely. So unlike *her.*"

We walked in silence. Humphrey was dragging his lame foot; it always tired if he walked fast, even for a little way.

I was exhausted and depressed. It was an effort to talk. I said, "We'll get you out of it somehow. I'll go and see her, offer her maintenance for the child. We must keep her quiet."

Perhaps it wasn't very tactful of me but I wasn't trying to be tactful. Humphrey said explosively, "Will, you're a cold fish. I'll be damned if I'll pay."

I said, "Don't be a fool. You've a family and a job."?

He said in his grand manner, "There are other jobs." Then he laughed suddenly and loudly as if he were really amused. "That sounds damn stupid, doesn't it? I'll say it and save you the trouble. I've already given her money. That'll count against me, won't it? Call it conscience money if you like. That's what it was."

I told him what Rose had said about the fifty pounds. He took it with an odd sort of calm. He said, "That's a pretty touch. It got you, didn't it, Will?"

He did not deny it and at the time, God forgive me, I thought this was odd. Later I wondered whether it might not have been the last edge of despair.

I said, "Where did you meet her?" not because it mattered but because I had to say something. It was no longer comfortable for there to be silence between us.

"I'd seen her in Somerhurst. Then, one night, she was in the Flamingo." He gave me a shamed, little-boy look and said, "You think I'm a fool to go there? I suppose I am. But I get so damn bored with all the nice people I meet. The Flamingo makes a change."

I said, "I don't give a damn why you go there."

He shrugged his shoulders. "All right. Anyway, she was there. She was with a friend. Another girl."

"What was she doing there?" I asked.

"I don't know. She said she'd never been there before. I should think that was true, she wasn't the sort of girl you usually see there. She was in London visiting her father. He's an old drunkard apparently, but she feels she ought to see him sometimes. He has two other children and she's fond of them. They have a flat in Kilburn."

"Does Piers know about her?"

He looked at me sharply. "He may. He was with me when I met her. I take him to the club sometimes—it's a nice cheap way of repaying his hospitality."

I said idly, "Do you have to stay there? With Piers?"

He laughed. "Where else would I get free board? Besides, I'm fond of him and he amuses me. You could never understand that, could you, Will? Or him? My precious half-brother who supports himself through his bookie and in other, less honest ways. Who speaks like an old Etonian, likes to be thought a blue-blooded Tory and lives rather less honestly than a barrow boy. It's a charming combination, Will."

For a moment he sounded unpleasantly like Piers himself. I said, partly to change the subject and partly because it was something that needed to be said, "You know I'm sorry about this. I hated having to tell you."

He grinned in the shadows. He sounded affectionate.

"Yes, Will. I believe you. Nothing would stop you from doing your duty, would it?"

He came with me to the station. We talked very little and we were both unhappy in each other's presence but he did not seem to want to go. He stood by the open carriage door, his face haggard in the dusty yellow light.

He said, at last, "Celia had lunch with me to-day. I thought there was something up. She kept starting to say something that sounded as if it was going to be important and each time she went as red as a turkey cock and stopped."

I said, "I didn't know she was coming. I told her I'd tell you about it."

"Thanks for that. She said was going to stay the night with her Aunt Milly. I thought it was a bit sudden; she usually plans these things months ahead with no end of fuss and bother."

Then the whistle blew and the train started to jerk. It moved a yard or two and stopped again. Humphrey shouted, above the noises of departure, "This is something I'll have to manage myself, Will. Don't you poke your lawyer's nose into it until I tell you to. It's my affair."

He sounded grim and his face had a fixed, white look about it that made me, for the moment, uneasy. But it didn't last long; 1 was beginning to have the edge of worry blunted by the thought of the long journey in the empty lighted train, and as it left the station my first and immediate desire was for sleep.

Chapter Three

I rang Celia the next day, at about noon. When I got the number it was answered by the maid. She said that Mrs. Stone had just telephoned to say that she was staying in London until after the weekend. No, she had left no message for Mr. Hunt.

Putting the receiver down I felt flat and more than a little angry. She might have told me what she was going to do; I had, after all, undertaken a peculiarly unpleasant job for her the day before. I told myself that it was foolish to be affronted. That there was no particular urgency about the business and if I had seen myself, sentimentally, as a knight errant, it was no fault of hers.

The days went by slowly with long, flat stretches of boredom. There was nothing that I wanted particularly to do and yet I was possessed by a curious and unfamiliar restlessness. My mother was returning from her annual visit to Scotland at the beginning of the weekend; I persuaded myself that I was lonely and missing her.

But when she did come I knew that I was wrong. After we had dined on Sunday night I was already regretting the month I had spent on my own and the lazy comfort of meals, eaten when I had wanted them, in the kitchen. Thinking like that gave me an uncomfortable sense of disloyalty; I reminded myself how pleasant the house was when she was there.

And yet the feeling did not go. I sat opposite her, watching her handsome, unlined face smiling at me as she drank coffee and smoked a cigarette and felt a quick constriction round the heart. We had sat together like this, evening after evening, for the last ten years. I wondered suddenly and with panic whether it would be the same for the rest of my life. I remembered that I had felt like this quite often lately. There was nothing specific that. I wanted; it was just that I was aware of missing something. It gave me an odd, unhappy sense of waste.

She talked, in her calm and pretty Scots voice, about her holiday in Edinburgh, and how, after standing in the sun for two hours, she had seen the Queen. She was an amusing talker and usually I enjoyed listening to her but to-night, somehow, I was bored. Her voice went on and on with bland assurance like the voice of an announcer on someone else's wireless and with the same deadly irritation.

I think I must have yawned because she looked at me with a small, reproachful frown.

"Are you tired, William dear?" she said.

The telephone rang and I got up to answer it. It was Humphrey. He sounded as if he were unsure of his welcome and it made him over-jovial.

"Is that you, Will? What are you thinking of us? I meant to ring you up but I moved in with Celia at Aunt Milly's flat and there never seemed to be a moment to do anything. You can guess what it's been like."

He sounded rueful. I said quickly, "It doesn't matter."

He cleared his throat loudly. "Look, Will. You are acting for us in this, aren't you? I mean you don't have to believe that your client is in the right before you act for him, do you?"

I said, "No, I don't." And then I hesitated. If I wanted to back out I could do so now. But I said, "Of course I'll act for you."

Humphrey said, "Thank you, Will. I wondered if you would see the girl. Go to her home, I mean."

I said, "I don't know what good it will do."

"Just to *talk* to her. For God's sake, Will, she knows I'm not the father of her child. If you tell her you've talked to me she might tell the truth. She *must.*"

There was appeal in his voice. I said, "And suppose she won't? If she gets an order against you, are you going to fight it?"

He said nothing for a moment. Then—"I meant it when I said I wouldn't give her any money but I've changed my mind. I talked to Piers. Oh, I know what you think of Piers. But he's nobody's fool. He said if she wouldn't come clean it would be better to pay her hush money to keep her quiet."

I said, "I told you that myself. Only not so vulgarly."

He laughed. Then he said, "We're treating you a bit rough, aren't we? Asking you to run our dirty errands and not even taking your advice?"

I said, "Don't worry. The advice will be on the bill." I didn't feel very friendly. I didn't try to pretend that I did.

I heard the door-bell ring and my mother, who had carried the coffee cups out to the kitchen while I was answering the telephone, walk along the hall.

I said, "I'll see the girl to-morrow. Shall I come in during the evening?"

Humphrey tried to persuade me to dine with them but I refused. I felt I had got the thing on to a strictly business basis and I wanted it to stay that way.

When I put the receiver down I heard my mother talking to someone in the hall. Then she came into the drawing-room, closing the door gently behind her.

She said, "I'm sorry, William. She says she must see you. Her name is Blacker—at least I think that's what she said."

I wasn't bored any longer. I went out of the drawing-room and into the study.

But it wasn't Rose. It was someone much older, a little, skinny woman in a coat of so dead and dull a brown that it was impossible to imagine anyone choosing it for any purpose other than camouflage. She wore a joyless hat and black, pointed shoes with cuban heels. Her eyes were watery and pale and stupid.

She said, "Mr. Hunt, is it? I'm dreadfully sorry. This is an imposition—on a Sunday night too—but I had to come and see you."

Her voice was carefully refined. She went on, "I'm Irma Blacker. I've come about my daughter."

Her mouth was set grimly but more with nervousness than anger.

34

It wasn't naturally a hard mouth. It was shapeless and a little silly; the mouth of a woman who is easily sentimental.

I said, "Rose?"

She nodded and then burst into speech, gabbling at me with worry. "Yes, Mr. Hunt. She's gone away and she hasn't come home. I couldn't believe there was anything wrong at first but it's five days now."

I remember that I felt quite cold. I said, "Did she leave home without telling you where she was going?"

She shook her head. There were little wisps of grey hair sticking out from under her hat.

"No. She went to London last Monday to stay with her father. She's my adopted daughter, you see, and she goes to see her father sometimes. Her real father, that is. My hubby's dead. She said she'd be back on the Thursday. When she didn't come and there was no letter or anything, I sent a wire to her father. He hadn't seen her. She'd walked out of the flat the night she got there and she hadn't come back. I thought she must come home—I waited till this evening and then I was so worried I didn't know what to do. I didn't want to go to the police—it's the disgrace and all the neighbours knowing about it. You can't keep these things quiet, you know. Not in a little town like this. And then I thought of you. I thought you might be able to help."

Her voice trailed into silence. She sat, smoothing the leather gloves on her hands and looked helpless and tired.

I said, with a heavy heart, "You may have to go to the police isn't there anyone—a relation perhaps—that she might have gone to see?"

"I don't think so. She hasn't got anyone. She got the children their supper on Monday night and went out. She didn't say where she was going. *They* weren't bothered when she didn't come back. They're like that. Rose has a friend who lives in the same house but she didn't know where she might be."

I said, "Mrs. Blacker, why should Rose run away?"

She looked frightened and ashamed. "That's why I came to see you, Mr. Hunt. Rose told me she'd seen you and that you knew about her."

I said, "She told you about the baby?"

The flush spread upwards from her sallow throat. She said, looking away from me, "It was only natural, wasn't it? I mean, you'd expect her to tell me. I suppose your Mr. Stone says it's not his baby. She showed me the letters he'd written to her. Dreadful letters. How a man in his position could bring himself to write such letters I don't know. Glorying in the wickedness of it all. He wouldn't have written to her like that if there had been nothing between them, now would he? I suppose he thinks that it can be hushed up. I'm not going to allow that, Mr. Hunt. Rose may have been a bad, wicked girl, but she's got her rights."

I said, "Mr. Stone doesn't deny that he was in love with her. He does deny that it is his child."

She said, with a kind of lumbering sarcasm, "Oh, he does, does he? I suppose I might have expected that. He can't prove it, though, can he?"

I said flatly, "No, he can't prove it."

She said weakly, "Then I hope you told him so."

I said, "When Rose told you about the baby, were you very angry with her? I mean might she have run away because she was unhappy?"

She became, then, uneasy and momentarily silent as though the memory of what she had said to Rose was not a pleasant one.

At last she said truculently, but with a note of pleading uncertainty, "You wouldn't expect me to be pleased, would you? After all it is so ungrateful. When she's had a good home and a decent Christian upbringing. I told her, and it was my duty to tell her, that she'd done something terribly wrong and that she'd be branded by it all the days of her life. No decent man will ever marry her now. I told her she'd behaved like a woman off the streets. She cried a good deal and said that it hadn't seemed wrong at all. I was right to be angry with her, Mr. Hunt. It was my clear Christian duty and no one will ever say I don't do my Christian duty."

Her face was scarlet with affronted righteousness. Then, quite

36

suddenly, her expression changed. She said with terrifying uncertainty, "She'll be all right, won't she? She's all I've got."

Her eyes swam with easy tears but the worry and the affection were genuine enough. The appalled anger I had felt the moment before departed and I was almost sorry for her.

I said, "If she hasn't come home by to-morrow, I think you should tell the police. They're kind, you know, and discreet. You mustn't worry about telling them."

She said, "I've never had anything to do with the police before." She spoke as if they were some kind of malignant disease.

I said, thinking of Rose, and knowing that I was involving myself finally, "I'll see them for you if you like. If she isn't home by to-morrow morning, let me know. I'll want a list of the things she was wearing and all that sort of thing."

She nodded dumbly. There was a stricken look on her face.

I showed her out and went back into the study and sat with my head in my hands. I thought of Mrs. Blacker and her narrow anger and the effect it might have had on an already frightened girl. Then I remembered Rose's fear and the feeling I had had that it was not only because of the baby that she was afraid. She had been possessed with fear.

I prayed, before I went to bed, that she would go home that night.

But she did not go home. The next morning Mrs. Blacker left a letter at the office. It was waiting on my desk. It was marked "Personal" in large letters, heavily underlined.

The Chief Constable was a golfing friend of mine. He was large and friendly and he greeted acquaintances as if they were his life-long friends.

He took notes of Rose's London address, her appearance and the clothes which, according to Mrs. Blacker, she was probably wearing. She had made out a list and enclosed it with her note.

Hartley said, "Small, slender, dark hair, black eyes, eighteen years old. Dark blue linen suit, white cotton blouse. Grey high-heeled shoes, grey gloves, white plastic handbag. You know, old man, girls like this disappear by their hundreds. They're always attractive or they sound attractive. Never a plain one, you'd think, till you saw 'em."

He sounded casual and un-caring and it annoyed me. I said, "This one was beautiful all right." He looked at me and smiled his jolly smile.

"Was she now? I hope I see her when she turns up."

"Do they usually turn up?"

"Lor bless you, yes. They've usually legged it to the seaside with the boy friend. Can't face the parents so they disappear for a week or so. Little blighters."

He doodled with clumsy fingers on the blotting pad in front of him. "There isn't anything else? No mole on the left elbow, or anything like that? Was she pregnant?"

I said, startled, "How did you know?" and cursed myself for a fool.

Hartley chuckled. "I didn't know. But that's often one of the troubles. Too coy to tell Mother. Or they've told Mother and there's been a royal row and they've hopped it. The family gets the wind up and comes to us. Afraid their erring daughter has thrown herself under a train. They rarely do, you know. Just go off for long enough to give Mum and Dad the fright of their lives. *Then* they'll be sorry. Childish instinct in us all."

I said, "It wasn't noticeable. Her being pregnant, I mean."

He tapped his teeth with his pen. "Then it doesn't rule out the boy friend and Brighton. I say, old man, you're taking this too seriously. How about some golf this afternoon?"

I said that I had to work for my living and he laughed in his breezy way and suggested a drink. We went to the nearest pub and stayed there for nearly an hour; afterwards I went back to the office feeling sleepy and cross. I reminded myself that I always felt like that if I drank in the middle of the day. I snapped at my secretary and she looked hurt about it, but I wasn't sorry. She was a superior young woman with a university degree which, so she appeared to think, relieved her of the obligation of being able to type.

I went home and sprayed the roses until dinner was ready. My brain felt sluggish and tired and I ate in silence while my mother made bright attempts at conversation. I knew I had behaved badly when I looked up and saw her bright, withdrawn smile. I tried to make amends by offering to wash up; she refused, as she always did, and left me feeling a brute and a boor.

When I got to the School Celia and Humphrey were in the drawing-room; the coffee tray was on a table between their chairs. The coffee cups were pretty, white with a green pattern; set out on the tray beside them were the liqueur glasses they had brought back from Venice. It was all very gracious and civilised; in the mood that had descended upon me it seemed a little self-satisfied and smug.

They gave me coffee and brandy and talked about the weather. Celia said that the hot summer meant a cold winter and had my mother ordered all her summer coal?

At last Humphrey said, "Will, did you see Rose?"

I told them, in complete silence, that she was missing. That she had been missing since the ninth of August.

Celia said, "That proves she was lying. She was afraid she'd be found out." No one said anything and she went on, "You believe she was lying, don't you?"

Humphrey said quickly, "I shouldn't ask him that. It's not his job to believe me. Only to get me out of a mess." His voice was amused but his eyes were not.

She stared at me with her blue, prominent eyes. "Will, do you think Humphrey is lying?"

Humphrey said, "Stop it, Celia. I know what he feels. Part of him believes me—the human part—because we're friends. The other part, the part that's a lawyer—and he wouldn't be any good to us at this moment if he wasn't a good lawyer—can't be sure that I've spoken the truth just yet. It's as simple as that."

It wasn't like that at all but I was grateful to him for trying to make it easier for me. He sounded bitter, though, and I knew I could not blame him. I would have given anything, just then, for a smooth tongue, but they were my friends and I could not pretend to them. I said, "She isn't the sort of girl you usually find in a mess of this kind. Humphrey loves you, Celia. He would say anything to save you pain. I can't altogether believe him when he says the child is not his. I'm sorry, I'd better go."

I got up, realising with self-contempt that my legs were trembling.

Celia was white round the mouth; anger made her look ugly and middle-aged.

She said, "Will, you're a fool. You've got tangled up in a lot of silly sentiment. Because she's pretty and young you think of her as a victim."

I said, "I really am sorry, Celia," knowing that I wasn't sorry at all. "But I'm not being sentimental. I don't necessarily believe the girl either. . . ." I stopped, knowing that I must sound absurd.

She said with a wild giggle, "Mr. William Hunt. Calm and judicial. Sitting on the fence not believing anyone. Haven't you any feelings at all?"

She broke, inevitably, into tears and flung herself down by Humphrey's chair, turning her face away from me. Humphrey put his arm round her shaking, thin shoulders and looked at me as if I were an enemy. "We're all a bit tired," he said. It might have been an apology; I think that perhaps it was intended to be. But his face was thin and hostile.

I left the house and drove home. I put the car in the garage and went for a walk. When I came back to the quiet house I felt very much alone.

I went to bed and thought about Rose. I tried to think about Humphrey, whom I dearly loved; but he was as distant as a stranger. I wondered if Hartley had been right about Rose. He was experienced in these things, and if he thought she would turn up then she would probably do so. I remembered her eyes (Hartley had not seen her eyes), black as pieces of coal and wide with fright.

I was almost asleep when the telephone rang. There was no extension upstairs; the only instrument was in the drawing-room. I dragged myself from my bed and went downstairs. I fumbled for the light switch and missed it and went across the dark room to the desk.

Hartley said, "Hunt, I'm sorry to bother you, old man. Were you in bed?"

I said; "I was. It doesn't matter."

He said, "I wouldn't have 'phoned, only it seems important. I wouldn't have known about it myself until to-morrow, only the wife and I were at a bridge party and I remembered I'd left my tobacco pouch at the station. So we dropped in on the way home and there was this report. It isn't complete, but it seems to fit the girl you told me about this morning. We can't be sure, of course, till she's identified, but there's one rather nasty touch."

"Yes?" I said.

"It's awkward. Very. Could you come down to the station?"

"Now?"

"I'm afraid so." He returned, momentarily and uneasily to his normal manner. "I know it's a fearful bore, old chap."

I said rudely, "Nonsense. Of course I'll come." I caught my shin against the table leg as I made my way across the dark room to the door. The pain of it bothered me all the time I was dressing and prevented me thinking about anything else. By the time I reached the station I was feeling very little except a rather unpleasant kind of excitement. Hartley looked very funny behind his desk, wearing tails, and with the scent of a good cigar still about him.

He said, "They've found a girl in the Grand Junction Canal. The part that's just off Maida Vale; they call it Little Venice, God knows why. The canal is fenced off but the boys get over the fence, of course, and as yesterday was Sunday they were there in strength. They go to fish, though I don't know what they expect to catch. Anyway, they found this girl, bobbing about under the bridge. She'd been there about six days, they think, but the medicos haven't finished with her yet. It takes about a week for a body to surface in the summer—maybe a bit less in this atrocious hot weather. Jennings says that she was most likely knocked on the head and pushed in the drink to finish her off—though they're not sure about that one yet. We'll know to-morrow."

I wondered, distantly, if I were going to be sick. I said, and my voice sounded a long way away, "You remember you said that the description might fit anyone?"

Hartley did not look at me. He said, "Not anyone. That was a bit of an exaggeration. This girl's the right age, right colouring and everything. But that's not the whole of it. They found her handbag. That wasn't in the water. At least, it had been, but not for long because the things inside weren't damaged much. It was hanging by its handle on a bit of an old tree that juts out from the bank—rather as if someone had seen it floating by, d'you see, and stuck it there. Like people stick gloves on a railing if they find 'em in the street."

I said, as if it mattered, "But they don't do that unless there's only one glove. One glove's no use to anyone. I should have thought anyone finding a handbag would take it to the police."

"Not the youngsters you get in that area, old man. Besides, there wasn't any money inside it when our people found it. I expect one of the boys found the bag, swiped the loose change and slung it on a tree for the owner to find when she came along. Not a dishonest boy, entirely, just one who reckoned be ought to have a reward for rescuing property from the canal."

I said, "What else was in the bag?"

"Cosmetics and an empty purse. Ration book with an emergency card for last week. Pair of spectacles—did she wear 'em, by the way? Handkerchief and a fountain pen without any ink in it. Return ticket to Somerhurst . . ." His voice trailed into silence and there was an uneasy feeling in the air.

The sense of unreality became acute. I said, "You're quite sure the bag belongs? To the body, I mean."

Hartley shrugged his shoulders. "How can we be sure yet? But it seems likely. And if it doesn't belong, what's it doing there?" He sighed wearily and made small shuffling sounds with his feet. Then he said, "Now I think you'd better tell me a bit about her. Why did you come to me in the first place? It's usually the relations who do that."

I saw, with a kind of remote surprise, that his manner had

changed. He was the police officer now and not my friend. His little blue eyes were cold.

I said carefully, "Her mother was upset. She asked me to come."

"But why?" he said.

The palms of my hands were sticky and I rubbed them down my trouser legs. I said, "Mrs. Blacker used to be a client of mine."

"Used to be?" said Hartley. "You know, you'll have to tell me all about it."

I fancied that his eyes looked a little less cold. Hartley said, "I'm not at all sure that I should tell you this. You are a friend of Humphrey Stone's, aren't you? You are his solicitor?"

My head was swimming. I said, "Yes, I suppose I am."

"You don't sound very sure?"

"Yes," I said.

Hartley relaxed a little, his untidy body sprawling in his chair. "It's all damned awkward. I don't like it. Stone's an important man and all that. We don't like making mistakes, you know, we like to be sure. There were some letters in the girl's bag. They were signed with his name and his address was on one of them. Of course they may be forgeries. We'll find that out in due course but it would simplify matters all round if Mr. Stone could be persuaded to tell us what he knows."

I said stubbornly, "I can't say anything until I've talked to my client."

"Which one? Mrs. Blacker or Mr. Stone? He'll take your advice, won't he?"

I said, "Are you asking me to make a statement?"

"Not officially. This is off the record. You should know that. I only want to know how much Stone comes into this."

I said, "All right. They're his letters. I mean, he wrote them. The girl was trying to say he was the father of her child."

Hartley eased himself cautiously from his chair as though his rheumatism was troubling him and walked heavily about the room. He said, "Trying a spot of blackmail, eh? Easy to say that she was lying, now she's dead." He whirled round to face me like an active elephant. "What d'you think? Think she was lying?"

"What I think isn't evidence," I said.

His eyes were very bright. "Of course not," he said. He sat down at his desk again and fiddled with, his pen. He said, "This is a beastly business. I hope to God your client knows where he was on the ninth of August."

I repeated his words stupidly. "The ninth of August?"

I thought Hartley was looking at me curiously.

He said, "That was the night she walked out of her father's flat and didn't go back. Your evidence. We haven't checked up yet."

I said, hedging wildly, "But she may not have been killed that night."

"No," said Hartley drily. "But it's reasonable to suppose that she was. Anyway, you needn't worry. Honest citizens don't knock young women on the head even if they are accused of fathering their brats. I expect Stone was a long way from Little Venice that night."

He was almost jovial now, the blue eyes twinkled.

I said, "He was in London. He was with me until quite late that night."

The twinkle went. "How late?" he said.

"I caught the last train home. At about eleven forty-five. He came with me to the station."

He muttered, not looking at me, "Well, I expect he can explain himself. We'll want to see him, of course. Was the girl a wrong 'un, d'you know?"

I said flatly, "I can't tell you. I don't think so."

Hartley said, "Mmm. It would make it a lot easier if she were. You'd better go home to bed. That's where I'm going."

He got up from his chair and came across to me. He looked a very old man, and tired. "They'll be sending a man from London to see Stone. Just a routine check, you understand. It's not in my hands, you know. Shouldn't really have told you all this to-night. Just that the girl had been found. I'm an interfering old buffer."

He drew his heavy eyebrows together and frowned at me. He said angrily, "Go home now and get some sleep."

I went home for what was left of the night. I would have to see

Humphrey in the morning whether Humphrey wanted to see me or not. And Mrs. Blacker. I thought of my own unwilling part in the business and I knew that I wanted to shut my mind to the rest of it. I didn't have to be involved; it was not too late to keep out of it.

Then, knowing that I would not sleep, I thought of Rose with an uprush of pity and horror. Poor, pretty Rose.

Chapter Four

The morning was hot; the terrace in front of the house was washed white with sun. The children rolled, naked, on the warm stone; their smooth brown backs glistened with health like silk. When I came up the steps they wriggled apart and ran to me, winding themselves round my legs.

Robin shouted, "Uncle Will, we're cannibals," and dug his baby teeth into my calf.

I said, "Get away, little beast," and held him off by the shoulders. His bones were small and delicate beneath my hands.

Willy said virtuously, "Mummy said we weren't to really bite." Robin flung himself backwards so that he was almost upside down and made a horrible face at his brother. Then he twisted himself right way up and said, "Uncle Will, I haven't many teeth to bite with. Jus' gums." He opened his mouth as wide as it would go and showed the gaps where the first teeth had fallen out, the hard white ridges where the new teeth were coming.

I said, "What teeth you have are sharp enough," and bounced him in the air. I was more fond of Robin than of Willy, my god-child, I suppose because he was so much more like Humphrey.

Willy came up to me. He said, solemn eyes large, "Uncle Piers is here."

Robin struggled to his feet. He said, in a shrill voice, "I don't like Uncle Piers. He's like a slug, all fat and slithery."

Willy said, "Shut up. He'll hear you. And you shouldn't say it, anyway. He gave you half a crown for your money box."

Robin grinned. "All right," he said. "Come on, Willy. Daddy said we could play in the gym this morning."

They went across the quad, their legs flying, and I watched them absently, wondering why Piers had come and feeling rather wretched at the thought of meeting him. Humphrey came out to meet me on the terrace. He looked tired, he had shaved himself badly and one cheek was cut.

He said, "Thank God you've come. The hounds arrived just after you rang me this morning. I must say it was a relief to be prepared. Not that they weren't extremely polite. There was only one man, really. A nice chap, rather dull. He had a sort of underling with him who didn't say anything, only flapped his ears." He stopped and added awkwardly, "I'm sorry about yesterday, Will."

It had always been an effort for Humphrey to apologise and knowing this, I was embarrassed because he felt he had to do so.

I said, "That's all right." I looked at the sunswept stone. "I went to see her mother," I said. "She's just off to identify the girl."

It had not been an easy interview. She had been angry, as though Rose's death were a personal insult, hysterical and genuinely stricken. Grief did not dignify her; it was impossible to feel anything for her beyond a certain conventional pity. I do not know why this should be so; that she had loved her daughter was certain, and yet I had not, at any point, been moved by her sorrow. Perhaps I had expected too much of her limited understanding; in her place I would have felt guilt-ridden and ashamed and because she did not, I blamed her for it.

Humphrey said, "Piers is here. He came this morning. I'd forgotten we'd arranged for him to come. Celia's fed up about it."

"I can believe it," I said.

Humphrey said irrelevantly, "She says he spoils the children. He gives them money and too many sweets. He doesn't mean any harm." I could not see Piers as a benevolent uncle and I said so. Humphrey looked at me sideways. "But he is desperately anxious for affection," he said.

We went into the drawing-room. Piers was lying back in an armchair, his fat legs spread out in front of him, his white hands folded across his stomach. His eyes were closed but he opened them as we came in.

"Good-morning, dear boy," he said. "You must excuse a very old gentleman. I like to cat-nap in the morning. Especially after the strain of a journey. And a policeman. Vulgar fellow."

I saw Humphrey look at him unhappily and Piers smiled broadly back at him.

Humphrey sat down. He said, "I'd better tell you what's happened, Will. They want to know about Rose. I told them my part of the story—I must say they were damn nice about it. They wanted to know about the night that you met me in London. I told them that I was with you until you caught the train. Then they asked me what I did after that, so I told them I took a taxi from the rank and sailed back to the flat. It took about twenty minutes. Piers told them that I got in at about ten minutes past twelve, so that was all right. They were very polite about it." He sounded faintly surprised.

"An unshakeable alibi," said Piers and grinned like a cat who has been at the cream. "They wouldn't dare doubt two such reputable gentlemen."

Humphrey said, "Oh, shut up." He looked miserable and weary. Piers looked astonished and closed his eyes. He said, gently, "Don't mind if I drop off, will you? I'm sure our William will be pleased to see me being as droner like as he always suspected." He added, softly, "Such a nasty, nasty old man, never done a day's work in his life, no sound public school values." He opened one eye. "That's how you think of me, isn't it, William?"

Humphrey put his head in his hands. "Don't listen to him, Will," he said.

I felt savage. I said, "It's almost impossible not to."

Piers sat bolt upright in his chair. His stomach drooped weightily on his knees. His eyes were scornfully bright. "I shouldn't be *too* nasty, dear boy. I've just pulled your client out of a nice little mess. Probably saved him from the hangman. A barbarous custom, hanging."

There was an unpleasant silence. I said, to Humphrey, "What the hell is he talking about?"

Humphrey said, with helpless anger, "He should keep his silly mouth shut. It isn't anything."

Piers raised an eyebrow. "Isn't anything? Come, come. Was it as little as all that?"

Humphrey glared at me. He said, "He's just given me an alibi. A false one." He looked defiant.

I said, "What do you mean?"

Humphrey's eyes slid away from mine; he had a look of Robin, caught out in a fib.

"Perhaps I was a fool. But I wasn't doing any harm, so was there any reason why I shouldn't make it clear that I wasn't? When Piers got here, this morning, just after you rang up, I told him about the whole thing. Then I got the wind up; we both did, a little. I took the easiest way out."

I was thinking that this was not new. I remembered other occasions when Humphrey had taken the easiest way out. He hated people to think badly of him; it had led him before into small deceptions, little lies. I had always thought it a harmless enough kind of vanity.

I said, "Well, what *did* you do after you left me?" I wondered why they should have assumed that it was the time after I had caught my train that was so important.

Humphrey sounded sullen. "Nothing much. That's the trouble. I went for a walk. It seemed natural enough then, but after I'd talked to Piers about it it sounded dubious, somehow. I didn't walk far. I got as far as Trafalgar Square and then my foot started to hurt like the devil and I took a taxi. I gave the man the address of the flat, but I didn't go all the way. I knew I shouldn't be able to sleep when I got back so I stopped the taxi in the Edgware Road and walked the rest of the way. It seemed a good thing to do at the time. I even passed by the bit of the canal where they found her. There's a low sort of bridge at the Maida Vale end where the canal goes under the road and I leant on it and rested my foot and looked at the water. This morning it seemed a bit too much of a coincidence for the police to swallow."

I said, "You bloody fool. You silly, bloody fool." My head started to ache; I could feel my sleepless night in my bones. I said, "We'll have to see the police and tell them this. It'll sound bad, but not as bad as if you leave them to find out on their own that you've lied to them."

Humphrey said, "Will, I can't do it. I can't prove that what I did was innocent."

"There's the taxi-driver."

"I thought of him. But it makes it worse. He put me down at the canal; he'll remember that if they find him. I paid him the fare all the way to the flat because I thought he might not pick up anyone on the way back. He'll remember that."

He was sweating lightly; little beads stood out on the bridge of his nose. I spoke slowly to him as I might have spoken to a scared child.

"Look, Humphrey. You can't get away with it. They'll find the taxi-driver. They always do."

Piers said, "But he might not remember the address. And even if they do find him and realise that Humphrey has been lying, it gives them time, while they aren't thinking of Humphrey as a murderer, to find the chap who did do it."

The words were brutal but he said them with a kind of deep earnestness that was quite out of character. Then he added, in his normal manner, "I'm only anxious that Humphrey shan't be accused of killing a little gutter-snipe. Bad for the family. I might even be asked to resign from my club. That's the kind of reasoning you expect from me, isn't it, dear boy?"

He smiled at me without cordiality. "You must really give me credit for some of the finer feelings. You haven't a monopoly of them, you know."

I said to Humphrey, "Are you going to tell the police the truth? If you don't, I can't help you."

Humphrey looked at me. He said, "Is this a bluff, Will?"

I knew it was no good. "Of course it is," I said.

Piers was smiling gently and it gave him an oddly malignant air. I wondered what reason he could have for persuading Humphrey to put himself in such an appalling position. He was no fool. He must know what he had done.

I said, "You know what you've done, don't you? You've made it impossible for the police, once they find out the truth, to believe anything he says. They're ordinary, fallible people. When they find out he has lied to them because he was afraid, is there any reason why they should look farther than this likely man?"

Piers said in a voice as dangerous as steel, "Do you think my brother murdered this little whore?"

I shook my head. Piers went on, the white lids drooping over his little eyes, "Who do you think murdered her, then?"

I said helplessly, "How can I know?" And then, "Why should you assume, anyway, that she was killed after I caught my train? Why not before?"

I thought, for a moment, that Piers was shaken. There was a look of uneasiness, almost of guilt, on his face. He looked at Humphrey and then at me. He laughed, and said, "Did I assume that? I don't think so. Surely it is only natural to want to account for the way that Humphrey spent his time?"

It didn't ring true and I wasn't quite sure why. Then Celia came into the room and said that I was wanted on the telephone. She said, "It's the Chief Constable. He's been trying to get you at the office."

"I haven't been there," I said. I went into the study.

Hartley said, "Is that you, Hunt? Got some news for you. They think she was hit on the head all right; there's a fracture of the skull. Water in the lungs and all that, so the canal probably finished her off, poor creature. Oh, and she wasn't pregnant."

I said, "Are you sure?" and he made an irritable sound at the other end of the wire.

"Of course I'm sure. We don't make mistakes like that. It was probably a bit of blackmail. She left her father's flat at about eight thirty that evening. We shall probably get a bit more detail on how she spent her time. Family not very productive, though. The father's a drunk. They don't know who her friends were, or anything like that. Don't seem to have taken much interest."

I managed to thank him before I put the receiver down. I went back into the drawing-room and told them what Hartley had said.

Humphrey got up from his chair and went to the window, his shoulders slumped like an old man's.

Piers looked at me. There was surprising malice in his voice.

"Well, well. I wonder what went on behind that vacant, virginal mask. She wasn't a fool, was she, though I must say she looked it? I was with Humphrey when we met her. She had another girl with her. She shed her quickly enough when she started to talk to us. Clever as a monkey, I shouldn't wonder. She flattered the old man beautifully—buttered my paws as if she'd been doing it all her life. I told Humphrey she was a bad one, didn't I, dear boy? He got quite indignant with me. Said I was a dirty, suspicious old man." He chuckled with what seemed to be genuine amusement. "Well, I am a dirty, suspicious old man. But they have their uses. So have I!"

"Had you seen her at the club before?" I asked.

"Bless you, no. Not been near the place since. Not up my street at all. I should think the girl went there a lot. It's not a bad place to pick up the youngster with money to spend. Of course she said she'd not been there before. She was quite the little lady, she didn't think it was quite nice. She looked sadly wistful, I remember, the little prairie flower in bad company."

He laughed and I said, "It may have been true. You've not much knowledge of innocence, I fancy."

I wondered why Piers was being so talkative all of a sudden and what he was trying to hide, under his chatter.

Piers said, "All right, Lancelot. Go on thinking your sweetly pretty thoughts." He got up and lumbered to the door; it was almost, I thought, a retreat.

Humphrey said, from the window, "Will, I can't believe it. I can't believe she lied about the child. Why should she? If she'd wanted money out of me she'd have got it just as easily by threatening to tell Celia about us. It's not like her, she wasn't that kind of girl."

I said, "I don't understand it any more than you do. But you must go to the police. It's the only thing you can do."

He shook his head and there was a stubborn look to his mouth.

"It's no good, Will. I can't. It's not as easy as all that." He looked wonderingly at me. "Will, she wasn't as bad as Piers tried to make out. She wasn't bad at all. She was quite incredibly young and sweet and innocent. She was *good*, Will. It wasn't just a pretence, I'd swear. She adored her brother and sister. Once, we took them to the Zoo together. They loved her, you could tell that they loved her." He smiled suddenly. "They called her Rosie and she didn't like it. She said it sounded common. She hated to be thought common."

His eyes were indulgent. He said, "Poor Rose. Will, isn't it awful that I shouldn't feel more than that? Six months ago, if she had died, the world would have ended for me. Does that sound too grand to be true? Now she *is* dead and I feel sorry and guilty, but no more than that."

He walked about the room as if it were painful to keep still. "Is this my fault? Would she be dead, now, if I hadn't fallen in love with her? We can't know, can we? I could have sworn, when I put an end to it, that she didn't really care; that she'd never felt anything for me that was more than a kind of flattered affection. But God knows what she really thought. Am I responsible, Will?"

I said, "I don't think it does any good to hate yourself. She's dead. You can't bring her back."

My head was aching badly and I wished I were alone. I tried to think about Rose and I wondered why she should have said she was going to have a baby if she hadn't been going to have a baby. Could she possibly have been mistaken about it? I had been so very sure that she was telling the truth.

Piers came into the room. He said, "Humphrey, Celia wants you in the gym. Willy's fallen off one of the bars. He hasn't hurt himself but he's bawling the place down."

Humphrey went and Piers walked to the cabinet where the drinks were kept. He poured himself a whisky and drank it. He looked at the empty glass and refilled it. I saw, and it surprised me, that his hands were shaking.

I said, "I'll have some of that whisky, Piers."

He poured me one without speaking. I said, "Piers, you knew an awful lot about this girl from just one meeting, didn't you?"

He put his glass down and regarded the smooth, white backs of his hands, his eyes half-closed. He felt one hand with the palm of the other as if to reassure himself that there was no stubble on the soft skin.

He said, "Dear boy, I make up my mind about people on a very brief acquaintance. It's a gift, you know."

There was nothing out of character in what he said. He was unbelievably vain.

Through the open window came a loud, anguished wail as Humphrey carried Willy across the quad. We could hear Humphrey's voice, light and cheerful and soothing; he adored the children and he was good with them. He brought the boy into the house and carried him upstairs. A door banged distantly, and the screams died away.

Piers said, "William, I think there should be a truce between you and me."

He eyed me speculatively and quite kindly. "You know, you mustn't expect too much of people. Perhaps I should be more specific; you shouldn't expect too much of Humphrey. Your own standards are intolerably high and most people fall short of them. If they are human, that is. And most of us are human."

I was irritated and a little dismayed by this unlikely speech. I mumbled something incoherent in reply. I think that he was, in all sincerity, trying to make a friendly gesture. And also, that he was trying to warn me.

Mrs. Blacker rang me up at the office just before four o'clock. Her voice came over the wire with a terrible, forced gentility.

She said, "Mr. Hunt, I really must see you. It really is most important."

I said, "Have you been to London?"

"Yes." The refinement of her voice cracked a little. "Will you come to see me, Mr. Hunt?"

I wished that I did not feel so appallingly unwilling to see her. I looked at the pile of work in my "In" tray and said that I would come straight away.

The street was across the level-crossing in the poorer part of the town. It was a decent enough street and very dreary. The houses were small and respectable and ugly. They were all on one side of the road; the railway was on the other and a fence separated the pavement from the line. It was tumbledown in places and children were scrambling through the gaps, yelling to each other.

As I got out of the car and opened the wooden gate a small boy said, "My teacher lives there."

He stared at me with bright, bold eyes.

"Does she?" I said. I had forgotten that Mrs. Blacker was a schoolmistress. The child did not answer; he put his grubby hand to his mouth and ran, giggling, to a group of small boys on the opposite pavement.

When I rang the bell Mrs. Blacker opened the door at once, almost as though she had been waiting for me in the hall. She was dressed drably in black and her colourless face was flabby and marked with tears.

I said, "I came as soon as I could."

She showed me into the tiny front room of the house. It was clean and airless and smelt of polished linoleum. There was a tray of tea on the table and a plate of Marie biscuits resting on a paper d'oyley.

I said, "Did they keep you long in London?"

She shook her head. Her mouth quivered a little. "Not very long," she said. "It was dreadful, of course. All those men asking me questions about Rose and knowing about the baby. It made me so ashamed, I didn't know where to put myself. They made me look at the things in her handbag. It *was* her bag, you see, the one I'd given her for her birthday. She'd wanted it, one of her friends had one just like it, she said. But of course we didn't know how it had got there, by the river."

"What do you mean?" I said.

She looked at me, her pale mouth a round, surprised O. Then she said, "Of course, you don't know. I had to look at the body. It was lying there with a sheet over it. They shouldn't ask decent people to do these things. Her hair was different, lighter and not so curly, Rose's hair was dark and sweetly pretty. They said she was young, not that you could really tell, but she wasn't a bit like my Rose."

Chapter Five

At first I was not able to believe it; later with a ridiculous sense of anti-climax I felt both relief on Humphrey's behalf and, for Rose, a new, sharp terror. If she was not dead, then where was she? If she was alive, why was her handbag lying near the body of the unknown, dead girl?

Mrs. Blacker offered me some tea and a biscuit and we sat opposite each other on cheap, chintz-covered chairs. She sipped her tea and nibbled her biscuit and talked about Rose. Or, rather, she told me what Rose had meant to her. She was not the sort of woman who ever talked about anyone but herself.

Rose, with her grandmother, had been billeted with the Blackers at the beginning of the war. The grandmother had died after a short illness and Rose had stayed on alone.

She said, "She was quite a nice little thing, you know, not rude or rough like some of the other London children. I wouldn't have kept her if she hadn't been nicely behaved, I had my own little girl to think of. My husband thought the world of Rose—he would turn in his grave if he could see what has happened to her. I used to think sometimes that he thought more of her than he did of our Peggy. That was why I was against it when he wanted to adopt Rosie. But he liked his own way and he'd set his heart on having Rose so I gave in in the end. Her parents were quite willing—they were glad to be rid of the responsibility if you ask me. Then a few months after we'd got the papers through my hubby was killed on the railway and Peggy too. It was dreadful for me, I was under the doctor for months with my nerves. Of course I was glad I'd got Rosie then—it was almost as though he'd known what was going to happen, wasn't it? She's never been like my Peggy of course, but she's a sweet girl really and a good daughter to me. I used to wonder sometimes if I spoiled her. My neighbour was always saying, `Mrs. Blacker, you think too much of that girl of yours. It isn't any good to her.'"

I wondered if she always talked as much as this. I said. "When did she start going to London to see her family? Had she kept in touch with them all along?"

She shook her head and little strands of dead-looking hair twitched free from their hairpins.

"Not really. It wasn't until she left school that she started to ask me about them. I'd never pretended that I was her real mother, you see, it didn't seem right. I let her go to see them and she met her little brother and sister—her mother was dead by this time—and she came home so excited about them that I hadn't the heart to stop her going again. Not that she did go very much until about a year ago. She left school when she was sixteen and went to work in a shop. She worked there for about a year and then she wasn't well. The doctor said it was anÊmia. He said it would be better if she had a part-time job for a bit, and so she worked for two or three days during the week. We had just enough to manage on, it was very hard for me, Mr. Hunt, after all I've been used to, but I don't complain. The Lord knows what's right for us. He giveth and He taketh away. That's what I always say."

Tears glistened in her pale eyes; she was easily moved by her own goodness.

She said, "Then, when she wasn't working regularly, she used to go to her father's about once a fortnight. She'd stay two or three days and come home again. I used to tell her she shouldn't go so often, but she was like all young girls, she had to have her own way."

Her face fell suddenly into lines of panic. "Mr. Hunt," she said. "Where is she? Why can't they find her?" The tea-cup rattled in her hand and she put it down on the table. "I've worried so," she said. "I haven't slept a wink for nights. Why doesn't she come home?"

I said helplessly, "There isn't anything among her things? A letter, or something like that?"

She said, "I don't think so. I've looked." She gave me an uncertain glance. "Would *you* look in her room, Mr. Hunt? I may have missed something."

I told myself that it was none of my business; that I would be well out of it. It was a job for the police and not for me. But I said, "If you want me to, Mrs. Blacker."

She took me up the narrow stairs to the upper floor. Rose's room was clean and bare, a child's room. The bed was neatly made up with a cheap silk cover, and a drunken-looking teddy bear lurched on the pillow. There was a shelf of schoolgirl's books and a crucifix hanging in an alcove.

Mrs. Blacker said, "It's a nice room, isn't it? Rose likes things to be nice."

There wasn't much to look at. There was a chest of drawers filled with stockings and undergarments and a drawer in the dressing-table for cosmetics. She kept her personal junk in an old chocolate-box tied with a red ribbon. The things inside were ordinary and a little pathetic, a child's hoarded treasures. There were letters, a few bits of cheap jewellery, the programme of a Christmas pantomime and a pretty curved sea-shell. There were several picture-postcards of Southend from a girl who signed herself "Sylvie." Mrs. Blacker said that she was the friend who lived in the same house as Rose's father.

She said, "My Rose didn't have much time for her. She's a common girl."

All the letters except one were from Mrs. Blacker herself. The last letter was written on thick, expensive-looking paper and the writing was unformed and uneducated.

It said, "Dear Rose, I hope this finds you as it leaves me, in the pink. The boys are well and send their love, especially you know who! I'm having a wonderful time, but then you know me. Ha, Ha. London is a wonderful place. When are you coming up again?"

The letter was signed "J" and there was no address. Mrs. Blacker did not know who the writer might be.

I asked her if Rose had many friends and she shook her head.

"She's a home bird," she said. "She hasn't many friends in the town. I don't like her mixing with the other girls at the shop—she's easily led, Mr. Hunt, and they aren't a very nice type of girl. She's great friends with Mary Arnold. The doctor's daughter, you know. Ever such a nice girl. And then of course she goes to church—we're Catholic, you know. Rose teaches in Sunday School."

I said, "She must have friends in London."

"I expect she has. She likes people to like her, Mr. Hunt. She gets quite unhappy if someone doesn't like her. She's a generous girl, too. Extravagant, really. She brings me a box of chocolates every Friday night—lovely boxes that cost quite a lot of money. She's done that ever since she started earning."

We went downstairs and into the sitting-room. There was a photograph of Rose on the mantelpiece and I wondered why I hadn't noticed it before. It was a large photograph in a silver frame. She looked very beautiful and gentle and young. There was a little self-conscious smile on her mouth as if she knew that she was pretty, and was pleased about it. In spite of the gentleness it was not a weak or stupid face. I reminded myself that it must have taken more than a little courage to go to see Celia that Sunday night.

I said, "Is there anything else that you can tell me? Was she worried about anything else, apart from the baby, I mean?"

She stared at me for a moment and then her face lost all its foolishness and became completely wretched. She wrung her hands. I had never seen anyone do that before and it was a quite unconscious, wholly pitiable gesture.

She said, "Oh, yes, Mr. Hunt. There was something else. My Rose—she was terrified half out of her mind."

She struggled for a moment and then she began to cry. I took her by the elbow and helped her into a chair. She cried for a while in a helpless, healing fashion and then she wiped her eyes and looked up at me.

Her voice had lost its grating refinement, she spoke more naturally and with a terrible anxiety.

"There was something wrong," she said. "Something had happened to her, I'm sure of it. It was when she was in London—the time before she disappeared. It was about a fortnight before, I suppose. She came back a day early. She didn't say why. She looked so queer, Mr. Hunt. She was white and ever so quiet and sort of listless. She acted quite normally most of the time but now and again, when she thought I wasn't looking at her, there was such a funny look in her eyes. A *dreadful* look, Mr. Hunt. A terrified look, the way a bird looks at a cat. Then she'd see me looking at her and she'd laugh and say something and act quite ordinary for a little while. When she told me about the baby I tried to think it was that that had been frightening her, but I knew in my heart that it wasn't. It was something much worse—something so bad that she couldn't tell me."

I said, "When did she tell you about the baby?"

"The day before she went to London, on the Sunday night. The day she'd been to see Mrs. Stone. I heard her screaming and went into the room. She was sitting up in bed and shouting and screaming at the same time. At first I couldn't understand what she was saying but after a bit it came clear. She was saying, 'Oh, the poor old man, the poor old man.' Just that, over and over again, staring at the wall all the time as though she saw something terrible there. Then she woke up and I asked her what was the matter. She told me about the baby and I was so angry with her. She was soaked through and her poor hands were cold as ice. Mr. Hunt—I'm so afraid . . ."

She looked weary and very old. For the first time I felt honestly sorry for her.

She said, "Mr. Hunt, will you try to find my Rosie?"

I could have told her that the police would do their best; that they were, in any case, far better equipped to find Rose than I. But I think that she trusted me; I know that I found it impossible to say that I would not help her. I do not think I realised, at that time, how much I wanted to find Rose for my own sake. It was not just because she was pretty and pathetically young; neither then nor later was I in love with her in any ordinary sense although

I was, I think, fascinated by the fact that Humphrey had been in love with her. She became, for me, not so much a real person as a problem that I had to solve, until, towards the end, I was completely absorbed in her. I do not know how this happened; I know only that it did.

I said, "I'll do what I can, Mrs. Blacker."

I tried, awkwardly, to express a little of the compassion I felt for her. I am clumsy at that sort of thing but I did my best. I tried, too, to hide the fact that I had become, suddenly, quite appallingly afraid for Rose.

I went straight to the School. I heard the chatter of voices in the drawing-room as I crossed the quad. Celia came out to me in the hall.

"We couldn't put it off, Will," she whispered. "It's not a party really, just a dreary necessity. All the bores together. Do you want Humphrey?"

She vanished into the room. When Humphrey came out he had a glass in his hand and he looked a little drunk. He closed the door behind him so that the noise was hushed.

I told him that Rose was not dead; except for a momentary look of relief he accepted it almost with apathy.

"Thank God for that, poor child. But unless she turns up pretty smartly, with the police knowing what they do, I'm not sure that it won't be too late for me. I've been thinking that I ought to resign." He looked round the hall and at the pretty, slender staircase. "God knows I should hate to leave."

I had never seen him so dulled, so completely without resilience. I told him not to be a fool. I said, "When she does turn up I should think the other business will be dropped. The police won't talk about the letters, anyway. I don't think you should worry."

It sounded, to my own ears, rather hollow comfort.

He said, "They found her bag?" He spoke wonderingly, half to himself, as if he had forgotten that I was there.

"There may be some quite simple explanation." As I said it I knew that it could not be true. I added, "You are sure you haven't seen her? Lately, I mean?"

He shook his head quickly and said, as if to change the subject, "You'd better go in, now you're here. The sherry's not bad, if you can stand the company."

It was hot in the drawing-room although the big windows were open. There were a lot of lilies in a tall vase in the corner and they gave out a waxy, churchyard smell. Everyone was talking very loudly and I wondered why middle-class voices should always sound so unpleasant in the mass. I knew most of the people in the room and disliked them; it was with relief that I saw Emily Sutro by herself in a corner, her short-sighted eyes blinking over her glass. I wondered why she had taken off her spectacles; I had never thought of her as vain. She was my aunt, my godmother, and the headmistress of the big girls' school in the town. I was very fond of her.

When I went over to her she peered up at me in a blind sort of way and smiled.

"Why, William," she said. "How nice to see you here. I didn't think you would be. We're all being got over—I should have thought you were too friendly with Humphrey for that."

I grinned at her. "I shouldn't speak so loudly," I said. "I'm only here by accident." I hesitated a little and then I told her about Rose, because she was uppermost in my mind and because I thought Emily might be able to help me. I told her that Rose had disappeared and that the police were looking for her.

She said, "Yes, I know. A dreadful business." Her eyes were sad as if she meant what she said. She didn't tell me how she had known.

I said, "She was at your school. What was she like? Can you tell me about her?"

She finished her sherry. "You'd better take me home," she said. "I'll say good-bye to Celia."

We walked through the empty School back to my car.

She said, "I'll do my best. But there are so many girls. One rarely sees them as individuals. The ones you notice are first of all the naughty ones and secondly the clever ones. It doesn't seem quite fair, does it? Rose, poor child, was seldom naughty and she wasn't clever either."

When we got to the car she took her strong glasses out of her bag and put them on. She said, "That's better. I don't know why I ever take them off. Let me see, now. Rose wasn't a particularly clever girl but she was a pleasant, pretty creature and we all liked her. She was suggestible, I should think, and easily led. But not a nonentity. She was quite good at acting, I remember—is this any good to you, Will?"

I said, "I'm not sure yet. Just keep on, will you?"

"Well then, she had a talent for acting. She even thought of making a career of it. She told me that when I talked to her form in their last year at school. It was the first time I had ever seen her really interested in anything. She said that her mother was against the idea and I advised her to talk it over with her and come to me again. I think that her idea of being an actress was wholly confined to the cinema, that the legitimate stage—what a curious phrase that is!—had simply not entered her mind. Anyway, nothing came of it. I think she got a job in a shop when she left school." She sighed. "I remember that at the time I thought it very suitable. You know, William, it is so difficult to know where a girl will be happiest."

I said, "Did she have many friends? It would help if I knew who her friends were."

She frowned. "I don't really remember. She was a friendly girl, of course, very eager to be liked. I think she was friendly with Mary Arnold the doctor's daughter. At least, they appeared to be friendly at school; whether it went any further I can't tell you."

"You can't remember anyone else?"

We had reached her house and I stopped the car. Emily made no move to get out; she was staring in front of her and I thought that she looked upset.

She said, "Yes, I can, William. This girl left before Rose did. It was rather unpleasant. We had to ask her parents to remove her. Her family left the town shortly afterwards."

I said, "Will you tell me about her?"

I thought she sounded reluctant. "I suppose it can do no harm. She was a wild sort of girl, lovely to look at. She was very gay and happy and very naughty. I think, if I hadn't been her headmistress, I might have found her rather attractive. As it was she was too difficult for us. Her parents couldn't control her and neither could we. She got mixed up with a lot of young hooligans from the town. Then she stole things from the cloakroom at school and in the end she had to go. I was sorry for her parents. They were nice people."

I said, "And Rose? How friendly was she with this girl?"

She said, "For a time, anyway, they were inseparable. Young girls form very sudden and violent friendships, you know, and Rose looked up to this girl. She had a great deal more vitality than Rose and I suppose it was natural for Rose to admire her. I remember that we wondered for a short time whether Rose had had anything to do with the stealing episode, the two girls were so close together. But I'm sure we were wrong. Rose wasn't that sort of girl at all. When it all came out she was terribly shocked and upset."

I stared ahead through the windscreen at the quiet road.

"What was the girl's name? I know so little about Rose. It might help."

She said unwillingly, "Her name was Jasmine Castle. I don't know where she lives. Somewhere in London, I think. I told you that her family left the town."

She looked pensively at her lap. Then she said, "Rose had been kept in one afternoon for some minor misdeed—nothing very serious, I'm sure, because she gave very little trouble. The next day we had a letter from her mother. It was a long letter, rather incoherent and not very well spelt. It was the sort of letter we are always getting from mothers. The gist of it was that Rose had had a difficult and unhappy childhood and needed very careful handling. I showed it to Rose's form-mistress and she said she thought it was Rose's hand writing. We looked at one of her note books and saw that the writing was identical. I remember that we laughed about it and decided to say nothing. I'm not sure, now, that we should have

65

done that. It was careless and casual of us. There must have been something wrong for the girl to have written a letter like that; perhaps we could have helped her."

I said, "I don't think her mother is a particularly understanding sort of person. Do you think Rose was unhappy?"

She was distressed. "How can I know, William?"

I saw her into the house and went back to the car. I sat at the wheel for a while feeling insignificant and useless and a little appalled at the task I had set myself. Then I drove to a public telephone box and rang my mother to tell her that I should be late home and that she was not to keep dinner for me. She sounded ruffled and as if she thought I was being inconsiderate.

I went to the Arnolds' house. There was a dreary little queue outside the surgery and I guessed that they would not have started dinner yet.

Mary Arnold was a fat, pale girl with a damp mouth. She wore a pink jersey that was too tight for her and a row of pearls. She sat with her knees spread out and she blushed when I spoke to her.

I was not allowed to see her alone. Her mother explained, for her daughter, "Yes, my Mally was quite friendly with Rose when they were at school, but it was only a childish friendship. It didn't go any further after they had left school. You see, Mr. Hunt, they weren't *quite* in the same class. I'm sure you'll appreciate that. It would have been different if she had been a secretary or something. A lot of very nice girls do secretarial work nowadays. But she worked in a shop. I don't mean that it wasn't very nice and suitable for her, but we have a position to keep up in the town. I'm sure you understand that, Mr. Hunt."

She gave a "we professional people" smile. Mary Arnold said, "*Oh, Mother*," and blushed violently, but her mother went on like a steam-roller.

"Mally is very kind-hearted, she didn't want to upset Rose. But she saw my point when I explained that Rose was not a very suitable guest for our little parties."

I was furiously angry. I would have liked to have told Mrs.

Arnold that she was as extinct as the dinosaur and just about as pleasant. I felt a sharp and angry pity for Rose. I thought, as I left the house, of the little snubs, the polite and careful withdrawals that must have shown her she was not wanted. I remembered that I had not asked Mary Arnold whether she had known Jasmine Castle; for a moment I toyed with the idea of going back and then dismissed it. It seemed so wretchedly useless. The chance that this other girl would know where Rose might be was as slender as thread. I told myself that no one but an inexperienced fool would think otherwise.

I drove the car slowly back towards the centre of the town. It was mellow and golden and still. Outside the School the remains of Humphrey's duty party were leaving. I saw Humphrey's head bent towards a lilac-coloured hat and then he looked towards the car and raised his hand as though he wanted me to stop.

I wondered, for perhaps half a second, whether I should see the signal. I wanted, more than anything else, to be at home and out of it for a while. I drew the car into the side of the road and Humphrey put his head in through the open window and said, "Will, the police have come back. They're indoors. Came in the middle of the party. A nice, auspicious time to choose, wasn't it?"

If he was uneasy he didn't show it. He stood back so that I could get out of the car.

"I don't know what they want," he said.

"Do you want me to come?"

"If you don't mind." He gave a short, crowing laugh. It was the way he always laughed when he was nervous. He said, "I have a feeling that I could do with a henchman by my side."

Hartley was waiting in the study; he seemed faintly surprised to see me, even a little uncomfortable because I was there. With him there were a sergeant and a plainclothes man from Scotland Yard whom he introduced as Detective-Inspector Jennings. It was all very polite and almost social.

The man from London said that they hoped Humphrey would reconsider his statement about the time he had returned to his brother's flat on the night of the ninth of August. He was a gentle, little man with a soft voice and nice, amused eyes.

Hartley added, and I think it must have been a little out of order for him to do so, because Jennings looked at him with a trace of mild reproof, that the woman who lived in the flat below Piers had made a statement to the police.

It was a friendly gesture merely; it was obvious that he didn't want to say any more. Later we found that the woman had been taking her dog for a walk and she had seen Humphrey going into the flat at about one o'clock or a little after. She knew Humphrey well and there was no possibility of her being mistaken. She had, anyway, no reason to lie.

Humphrey looked at me and then at the policeman. His eyes were blank and amazed as though, he felt that this could not really be happening to him. He said, in a low voice, "I'm sorry. I'll tell you the truth now. It was stupid of me to try to avoid trouble."

He gave me a wry kind of grin and explained, a little haltingly, what he had really done.

It sounded bad, bad and lame. Hartley was staring at his boots and Jennings watched Humphrey in a quiet, inquiring fashion that made my heart sink. He looked like a kindly schoolmaster watching a small boy catch himself out in a lie.

I said, "But I understand that the dead girl is not Miss Blacker. If that is the case then my client has been unwise in not making a correct statement before, but surely there is not more to it than that?"

Hartley growled something under his breath and then said hastily, "Hmm. It's not as simple as that. We have some other evidence." He glanced at Jennings who shook his head with a barely perceptible movement. Hartley went on, "We have reason to believe that Miss Blacker knew the dead girl. They were seen together."

I said, sensing disaster, "The girl has been identified, then?"

Jennings said, "She was a young woman called Jasmine Castle."

After that there was an unreality about the rest of the evening. Humphrey was asked if he would go down to the station to make a statement. It was almost a social invitation.

We drove to the station. I took Humphrey and Jennings in my car and on the way they talked, casually, about the countryside.

The policeman said, "This is good walking country, isn't it? I used to like walking when I lived out of London. I'm in Harrow now, you have to get out a goodish way before you find a stretch that isn't built on."

He seemed a decent sort of man, disposed to be friendly.

At the station they let Humphrey write out his own statement on a special form which had the usual printed caution at the top. Humphrey was rather surprised that he was allowed to do this. He spent a long time on the statement, staring for long periods at the white-washed wall in front of him. The station sergeant brought up cups of sweet tea.

When he had finished writing the Inspector read the statement out to him and he signed it and was told he could go home. We drove back to the School in silence. Celia was waiting for us in the drawing-room, surrounded by the wreck of the party. We told her what had happened and she said, "Oh, my darling." Then she cried a little and clung to Humphrey. She was very indignant with the police. She kept saying, "But now you've told the truth it'll be all right? They must understand why you didn't tell it in the beginning."

Later she went to the kitchen to make a cup of tea; Humphrey had suggested that she should do so and as soon as she had closed the door behind her he said urgently, "Will, I told them the truth this time. It will be all right, won't it?"

A jumpy tic had started at the corner of his right eye.

I said, "I hope so."

He looked at me queerly; the twitch at his temple made him look ludicrously sly.

He said, "Will, you'd better know the rest of it. I'd have told you before only it sounded so damned queer." He stopped and a painful flush coloured his face but he stared at me quite steadily.

"Go on," I said.

He said, in a rush, "I saw Rose that evening, Will. I didn't think there was any need to tell you. Not because it didn't matter but because I was rather ashamed of it."

I said, as calmly as I could, "Did you arrange to meet her?"

He nodded. "I'd left a note for her at her father's flat. I'd been thinking about the baby. I felt badly because I hadn't answered her letters. It *wasn't* my baby, Will, but I felt responsible. She'd nobody much to help her. I don't know what I thought I was going to say to her; I had some vague idea of trying to find some way that I could help her without letting Celia know. It seems funny, now, but I was desperately afraid that Celia would find out.

"Anyway, I said that I would meet her at about half-past eight. I asked her to be out in the street and waiting for me. I wasn't too keen on going to the flat.

"When I got there she was in the street and she had another girl with her. I think she'd brought her along as a sort of protection. Rose was shy and queer—of course she'd been to see Celia by this time, though I didn't know it. As soon as we met she started to explain that she couldn't have dinner with me because she'd arranged to go out with some friends. She was very jittery and the other girl kept chipping in to say that it was quite true about this other engagement as though they thought that I might not believe it. . . .

"I felt a bit of a fool, gossiping on the pavement, so I took them into a pub and bought them a gin apiece. We stayed there for about half an hour, I suppose. It wasn't very pleasant, we hadn't anything to say to each other and I couldn't say any of the things I had meant to say because of the other girl. In the end they said that they had to meet these friends of theirs and they went off together. I stayed in the pub for a bit and drank a bit more. After that I went to a Lyons and had something to eat and then I went to the Flamingo. You know the rest."

He hesitated and then he said, "You know, Will, I've been a prize ass, but nothing more than that."

He grinned at me boyishly, and for the first time in my life I though his smile was irritating and silly. It was all so plausible, I thought, too smooth and easy. I was conscious of being disloyal and I hated myself for it, but I could not change the way I felt.

70

Humphrey had been so honest and open—almost like a caricature of a man being honest and open, making a clean breast of it. He even looked, I thought, quite pleased with himself.

I said, "This other girl. Did you know her name? Would you recognise her again?"

Humphrey's eyes were as dead and cold as the windows in an empty house. He said, "I shan't get the chance to recognise her. It was Jasmine Castle."

Curiously enough I felt nothing, not even surprise. I said, "You knew her, then?"

It was impossible to tell what he was thinking. He said, "I'd seen her around. In the Flamingo and with Rose."

"What was she like?" I said. It was a polite, social conversation.

He said calmly, "She was a striking creature. Not beautiful, like Rose, but with a lot of life about her. Big, soft mouth and a lot of movement in her face. She laughed a lot." His whole face glowed suddenly with anger. "I think she was a bitch," he said.

I said, "How well did you know her?" His face became shut and guarded.

"Not well," he said. "She was just one of Rose's friends. Perhaps I shouldn't have said that she was a bitch, perhaps it was unjust. I thought that she was a bad sort of friend for Rose."

I did not think that he was speaking the truth and I felt a kind of bleak despair that he should have to lie to me.

I said, "You should have told all this to the police. Why didn't you?"

He said blandly, "They didn't ask me."

I said, with brutal intention, "You can't get out of it quite so easily, you know," and it seemed to me then that the words which I regretted as soon as they left my mouth had an unpleasantly prophetic feel about them.

Chapter Six

He stared at me for perhaps a full minute, the skin stretched taut across his cheekbones and his eyes hard and angry and very bright. I had no idea what he was thinking.

Then his mouth twisted suddenly into quite unfamiliar lines of bitterness and anger.

He said, "Why the hell won't you believe me? D'you think I killed that girl? Are you shocked because of Rose? I know the answer to that one. You're shocked to the depths of your miserable little soul. I haven't lived up to your idea of me, have I? The nice, upright English gent—the perpetual Boy Scout. I honestly believe that's how you thought of me. You've no imagination, Will. No ordinary, human failings either. The shabbiest little bank clerk who pinches the barmaid's bottom when his wife isn't looking has more humanity than you. You don't *want* anything beyond your narrow life, do you? That's what sends me round the bend. You couldn't understand how I felt about Rose, not in a thousand years. You think I should be ashamed of myself; you think the whole affair was mean and underhand and dirty. It wasn't like that at all. It was one of the best things that ever happened to me. For a bit life wasn't circumscribed or sham, it had meaning and purpose. I'm glad I was in love with her, even now. You think I'm mad, don't you, Will?"

His hands were shaking; he glared at me as though I were his mortal enemy.

I said, conscious of nothing beyond a sick desire to hit back, "I don't think you're mad. I think you have an enormous capacity for self-deception."

He shouted at me, "Oh, God, how I hate your prissy mouth," and he went out of the room and banged the door.

I felt as I had felt all these years before when I had quarrelled with Piers, ashamed and cold and deathly sick. I wanted to leave but I told myself that it would be running away.

He was back in under ten minutes. He was carrying a tray in his hands. He said, "Celia's all in. She's gone to bed. Have some tea?"

He didn't look at me; he put the tray down on the table and poured out two cups with great concentration. Then he brought me one of the cups and said, "Will, can you forgive me?" He looked humiliated and tired. I tried to forget how I was feeling. It wasn't important.

I said, "You know you can say what you like to me."

He smiled with affection and, I think, contempt. He said, "Poor Will." Then he grinned. "Perhaps it's all for the best. Now you know how worthless I am, so don't waste your pity. I'm not worth anyone's pity. In fact it'll be best if they hang me and have done."

I thought, for a moment, that he was being deliberately theatrical but he wasn't. His nerves were stretched so tight that the most melodramatic words came naturally to him. He began to talk in a strung-up, garrulous fashion and everything he said was permeated with a sudden and maudlin self-pity that I found more embarrassing than all the abuse he had flung at me. He said that he was a hypocrite, a sham and a cheat, that he had behaved unforgivably and that he didn't deserve to live. He went on in the same strain, vilifying himself, hating his own actions and emotions until I could no longer look at him. It seemed to me, then, the last depth of horror that a loved person could be reduced to this abject self-destruction.

At last, because I could bear it no longer, I said, "Stop it, for God's sake. It helps no one. And I find it—despicable."

It worked. He stopped and looked sheepish and exhausted.

I said quickly, "You're talking like a fool. You should have told the police that you knew Jasmine Castle. It was stupid and dangerous not to. But that's all. They won't think that you murdered her because you saw her once or twice."

He said simply, "But I had plenty of reason to kill her, Will. She was blackmailing me."

There are moments when everything becomes clear and sharply drawn, moments that stand out in memory like three-dimensional figures against a flat background. I can remember now everything about that moment; the exact pinkish colour of the light, the pale patch in the carpet where a stain had been removed, the single cobweb strand that hung from the ceiling and moved gently in the breeze from the window. Humphrey's back was to the light, his head was tilted towards me at a slightly enquiring angle as though he had just asked a question and was waiting for me to answer it. There was a small smile on his thin mouth, a timid, almost conciliatory smile.

I said, "Hadn't you better tell me about it now?"

He limped across the room to the mantelpiece and took a cigarette out of the box and lit it carefully, holding it delicately and unnaturally between his fingers. He smoked very seldom; somehow the gesture added to the unreality of the whole thing.

It had begun after the affair with Rose was over and ended. He had been unhappy and drinking a great deal. He had been in the Flamingo one evening and Jasmine had asked him to buy her a drink. He was alone and bored and they had several drinks together. Then she said that she wanted to talk to him and suggested that they leave the club. She had seemed excited about something as though she were playing a secret game. They had left the club together; it was late and the streets were empty.

He said, "We walked for quite a while before she came to the point. I didn't mind walking, it was a nice enough night and she was an attractive creature—warm, and sort of *glowing*. I don't know what we talked about, although we must have been talking because I remember that she stopped suddenly in the middle of a sentence and said that she knew Rose. That Rose was her best friend. That brought me up with a bit of a jolt. I think that I was still in love with Rose just then. I wondered what she was getting at, and then I thought that she couldn't know about me because she went on to talk about Rose quite naturally and simply as though she wanted me to know about her. No more than that. I can't remember exactly what she said but it was something to the effect that Rose was extraordinarily pretty and that all sorts of people fell in love with her but that this hadn't made her catty and horrible at all because she was naturally so sweet-natured and innocent. 'Innocent' wasn't the word she used—she said 'a bit wet'; but she said it affectionately and not at all contemptuously, and 'innocent' was what she meant. I think that she was quite sincere in all she said; she seemed a very likeable sort of person. By this time, d'you see, I had begun to think of her as a person and not just as a pretty girl I had picked up in the club.

"That's why it was so much of a shock when she asked me for ten pounds. It was so unexpected that I couldn't believe I had heard her properly. I suppose I must have gaped like a fool because she laughed and said, for the second time, 'I want you to give me ten pounds. If you don't, I shall tell your wife about Rose. She won't like it, will she? I mean, it isn't as if Rose was a nasty sort of girl. She was ever so unhappy when you gave her up. It wasn't fair to do it so suddenly, you know.' She had a pretty voice, I remember, low and sort of gentle. It didn't change tone one bit. I was quite sure she meant what she said."

He gulped at his tea. I said, "Did you give her the money?"

He nodded. "It didn't seem that I had much alternative. After all, everything was over by this time and there was no point in having a showdown with Celia. It wasn't only that I was scared of what she would say, I was still pretty unhappy about it all and I felt I couldn't bear to have it dragged out into the open. Besides, Jasmine managed the whole thing with such an air of *mischief*, almost like a child playing a game, that it didn't occur to me that she would carry it any further. We were in a deserted street in the middle of the night. I felt that if she were experienced in that sort of thing that she wouldn't have tackled me there. I might have given her a nasty time. I was quite wrong, of course. She wasn't frightened of me; I don't think she was capable of being frightened of anything. Afterwards that seemed rather alarming. People without fear are somehow so inhuman.

"She asked me for more money, never more than ten pounds and once it was only five. If she had asked for more I might have gone to the police. She turned up when I wasn't expecting her, once at The Odd Flamingo and several times at Piers's flat. She didn't come to the flat, she hung about in the street and waited until I came out. She was always quite blatant about the money; it was a straightforward commercial transaction as far as she was concerned. She always smiled and thanked me very nicely when I gave it to her. I got so that I hated her smile. It was so blandly unselfconscious and full of young, white teeth like a toothpaste advertisement. Will, several times I could have killed her when she smiled at me."

He was trembling like an animal driven into a corner. He had lost his usual air of buoyant youth and looked what he was, a badly scared middle-aged man. I was sorry for him, but in a remote, detached way that did not affect me deeply.

He said, "When the police find out about this they'll be sure I killed her."

I said, surprised that I could think coherently still, "But that evening—when she was killed—I'd told you that Celia knew about Rose. She couldn't blackmail you any more, you would have had no reason to kill her."

He said slowly, "But I might have killed her first. I'd seen her, with Rose. I didn't know then that Celia knew."

I said, "Did she say anything? Ask you for money?"

He shook his head. "No, she didn't. Rose was there all the time, you see, and I don't think Rose knew about it."

I said, "Why shouldn't she have known?"

He looked dazed. "I don't know. But it isn't in character, somehow. Rose was honest and gentle and sweet. I don't think she was capable of that kind of shabbiness. Perhaps I'm only clutching at the last shreds of illusion. Not a pretty picture, is it, Will?"

He sat down, his hands on his knees and stared at the floor. He said, "Will, there was something badly wrong with Rose that night.

She barely opened her mouth in the pub. She never talked much in the ordinary way but that evening I got the idea that she was *afraid* to talk. She looked wretched and rather ill; and when she *did* say anything she looked at Jasmine first as though she was wondering whether it was all right for her to speak. I think she was scared of Jasmine. Perhaps that's the wrong word. Sort of hypnotised by her."

I said, "If she'd been involved with Jasmine in this blackmailing game she'd spoiled it all by going to Celia hadn't she? Perhaps they'd had a row about that."

He looked at me in a puzzled way. "No. She didn't act as if they'd just had a row. It was more important than that. I know that, though I can't explain why. I got the idea that she was frightened of something that, they'd arranged to do. She kept looking at her watch and when Jasmine said that they would have to go she looked at her in a terrified sort of way and said wouldn't they be rather early? I think that she'd have given anything to stay in the pub but Jasmine carted her off in a masterful fashion. She said that they mustn't be late."

"You've no idea where they were going? Or who the friends were that they'd arranged to meet?"

He grinned faintly. "If I knew that I shouldn't be in such a muck sweat now, should I?"

He got up and walked about the room, his hands in his pockets and his neck thrust forwards from his shoulders. Then he swung round to face me with a look of imploring agony.

"Will, suppose she doesn't turn up? Suppose she's dead. Suppose no one saw them, after they left me at the pub? Any jury would convict me."

I said roughly, "Don't talk like a fool. Of course she'll turn up. Anyway the police won't take any action until she does. She's their most important witness, remember. I don't think you should worry overmuch."

But he was beyond argument of that kind. He was deep in his private hell and nothing that I could say could reach him there.

His eyes were feverish and shining; I think that he was near to tears.

He said, "Can't we look for her? We can't just wait."

I was very tired. I said, "There's no need to wait. I could see her family. They must know something about her."

He shook his head. "Her father drinks and the aunt doesn't care about her. I think Rose was afraid of her. I saw her once—a savage-looking bitch in a Salvation Army uniform. They live in a nasty little hole in Kilburn. I went to the flat once when no one was there but Rose. It stank of meanness and poverty. There was a girl who lived in the flat below and I think Rose was quite friendly with her at one time. She was a dreary little creature. Quite young, I should think, but it was difficult to tell because she had made-up with a trowel. She was with Rose the night I met her at the club—I think Rose dropped her after that night. They might know something at The Odd Flamingo. And Jasmine Castle's parents—wouldn't they know something about Rose?"

He was speaking disjointedly, clutching at straws.

He said, "Will, you must help me. I shall go mad."

I had never before heard such helplessness and despair in his voice. I had loved and admired him for so long that it should have touched some spring of pity in me. And yet I felt nothing but horror and a kind of disgust, not only with Humphrey but with the whole sick world. I think that if it had not been for Rose I would have dropped the whole business then and there.

I went to the police station early in the morning, before I drove to London. I saw Jennings. They had allotted him a narrow, sunless room at the back of the building. He was polite and friendly and anxious to be of service. He listened to me with the right side of his face turned carefully towards me as if he were deaf in the other ear. He had a thin face with more lines in it than was natural for a man of his age. His eyes, as he smiled at me, were not amused, but sad.

He said, "Of course you are anxious to find the girl, Mr. Hunt.

We are all anxious to find her. If you can help us in any way we shall be grateful."

His manner was diffident but he sounded like a man who knew what he was about. I felt, even then, that underneath the gentleness he was both hard and sure. In a curious way, although he couldn't have been nicer or more obliging, I found him disconcerting.

The little girl said, "Mrs. Castle's upstairs resting." She spread her fingers over her mouth and giggled at me. She was a fat, freckled child, very plain.

I said, "Can I see her?" and she nodded her head and eyed me speculatively, with a cold adultness. "Are you from the papers? There's been a lot of men from the papers." Then she giggled again. "Mum says Miss Jasmine is dead and the worms are eating her."

Someone shrieked from the interior of the dark house. "Beryl, come away from that door." A ferret-like woman appeared from the end of the passage.

"D'you want Mrs. Castle?" she said. "If you'll step in, I'll fetch her." She turned on the child with ferocity. "Get back in the kitchen or I'll tan the hide off you," she said. The child giggled and vanished and I was left in the cold hall with the blinds drawn and the door closed.

When Mrs. Castle came down the stairs I was at once made aware that this was a house in mourning. She was dressed from head to foot in deep and tragic black. She was a big, dramatic woman and she must once have been quite exceptionally handsome. In the dim light she was handsome still. Only when she came close did you see that her eyes were no longer very clear and that there were crow's feet round them. She brought with her a heavy, stale smell of whisky.

I made my short, conventional speech of sympathy. I said that I was distressed to be intruding on her at this time. She hiccuped a little and said "Pardon."

She took me into a back room where the blinds were up and the windows open to the summer. Her husband sprang to his feet when she came in and fussed anxiously about her. He was a small, shy man with a cultivated voice. His face was yellow and dry like the faces of men who have spent their time in the East and the suburban room was full of ebony elephants and Benares brass.

I told them that I was looking for Rose.

Mrs. Castle said, "Such a lovely girl. I do hope she'll be all right. My Jasmine was so fond of her." She wiped her eyes with a large, black handkerchief.

Her husband said in his nervous, cultured voice, "You'll understand, I'm sure. In the middle of our own tragedy. . . . We'd almost forgotten the poor child."

I said hastily that of course I understood.

He went on, "She was our only one, you know. We have been hit very hard—very hard. To lose a child, and in such terrible circumstances, too—one finds it difficult to believe it has really happened."

Mrs. Castle looked like a tragedy queen. Her hair was dyed and she was growing old but she still had a kind of assurance, almost arrogance, about her that the possession of beauty brings. I wondered if Jasmine had looked like her.

She said, "The gentleman wants to know about Rose. Not about our darling."

She smiled at her little husband with an affectionate, slightly tipsy smile.

He said, "Yes, yes, of course," and blinked his eyes at me. "She came here quite a lot. We encouraged the friendship. Rose was a good influence. Jasmine was inclined to be wild and headstrong; she'd made some friends in the past that we hadn't liked at all. But Rose was different. So gentle and kind. And religious, too. We aren't Catholic ourselves, of course; I'm ashamed to say that we don't practise any religion."

Mrs. Castle said, in a deep voice, "I always say that it's the way you live that matters. Not going to church."

I said, "Do you know who their friends were? Where they spent their time?"

Mr. Castle said, "I believe they used to go quite often to a little club in London. Jasmine told us that there were a great many other young people there. We thought it sounded very nice and suitable. The club was called The Odd Flamingo. We shouldn't have liked Jasmine to go there on her own, perhaps, but as she went with Rose, we were sure it was all right. She was such a sensible girl, and nice-minded."

I said, "Did you know any of the people they met at the club?" I didn't think it was any use; these people seemed so oddly detached from the world.

The Castles looked at one another. Mr. Castle said, "No, we never met any of their young friends. Of course they were always laughing about some boy or other in the way that girls do but I don't remember that they mentioned any names."

Mrs. Castle said, "What about the old man? The one that died?"

Her husband said, "Oh yes. I came in one morning when they were here. Rose was crying. I asked her what was the matter and she said that an old gentleman who used to go to the club was dead. She was a sensitive child, you know, and she took things to heart. She was very upset; I found her distress rather touching. Jasmine was rather cross with her—she hadn't much patience. She took Rose upstairs to her bedroom to wash her face and I heard them quarrelling. I remember I thought Jasmine was being a little unkind to Rose."

Something stirred uneasily in my mind but I couldn't pin it down.

I looked at the quiet little man and the nice, drunken woman. I said unhappily, "You said your daughter was a little wild. Had she ever been in trouble with the police?"

Mr. Castle got up from his seat and went across to his wife. He took her large hand tenderly in his little paw. He said, "I'm afraid she had. She wasn't really a bad girl, you know, only wilful. She liked excitement and adventure. She was once on probation for stealing things from a shop. She didn't need the things she took; she'd never wanted for anything, had she, my dear? She promised us, when it happened, that she would never do it again."

I said, "Do you think she could have led Rose into bad company?"

He looked at me with puzzled eyes. "I suppose it is possible. Perhaps we were selfish. We were so glad, for Jasmine's sake, that she was friends with a nice girl like Rose. We never thought that she might do her harm." He looked sad and rather humble. I hoped that they would never know that Jasmine had been a blackmailer.

Mrs. Castle got up and went to the mantelpiece. She took down a photograph in a cheap frame.

"There's my Jasmine," she said. "And that's Rose with her."

It was an enlarged snapshot of two girl in summer dresses, sitting on a rug. They were looking straight at me and laughing as if they had been laughing together at some private joke when the camera had caught them unawares. Jasmine was very like her mother. She was a bigger girl than Rose with a lively, sensual mouth. They looked very pretty, bright and young.

And one of them was dead now, and the other missing.

When I left the house I was hot and sticky and tired. I drove back into London and down on to the Embankment. I parked the car and bought an evening paper. There was a small, cool breeze from the river and the surface of the brown water foamed with yellow curds. I leaned on the parapet and opened the paper.

The photograph of Humphrey was half-way down the front page. It was small and not very clear but it was quite recognisable. Later I discovered that it was a copy of one that had appeared in the local paper when he had been appointed to the School.

Underneath it said that the police were anxious to interview Mr. Humphrey Stone in connection with the dead girl who had been found in the Canal in Little Venice. It said that Mr. Stone had made a statement to the police that morning and had later left his home without leaving an address. It said that Mr. Stone was the Headmaster of Somerhurst School. He had served in the Royal Armoured Corps during the war and had been awarded a D.S.O. for gallantry.

Chapter Seven

Celia's voice was thin and distant and faintly unreal. She sounded not so much despairing as thoroughly bewildered. She had not seen Humphrey the night before; she had slept as soon as she had gone to bed and when she woke he was not in the room.

He was not in the house. The drawing-room smelt fustily of whisky and tobacco and the sofa was rumpled as if he had spent the night there. She had been puzzled but not worried, she had opened the windows and straightened the cushions and picked up the glass and the empty bottle. I think she had been concerned that the maid should not find them there.

He had come in when breakfast was over; she had heard the front door slam and his footsteps running upstairs. He had locked himself in the bedroom and did not answer when she asked to be let in. She had talked to him through the shut door, half angry and half alarmed, until he opened it. He was unshaven and looked ill; he had stared at her as if he were not quite clear who she was. She had asked him what was the matter and he said that there was nothing the matter and would she go away and leave him alone? He had waited, quietly and politely, for her to go.

She had not seen him again. She had not gone near the bedroom for some time for fear of disturbing him, and when she did, he had gone. He must have left the house almost immediately because the children had played on the terrace when they had finished their breakfast and they had not seen him.

Jennings had arrived later in the morning. She had asked him why he wanted Humphrey and he had told her that he had been to the station earlier and made a statement. He had told them all that he knew about Jasmine Castle. He explained, quite gently, that Humphrey had been asked not to leave the district without telling the police; Celia thought that Jennings had not believed her when she said that she did not know where he was.

She shouted suddenly, in a burst of panic so that I had to hold the receiver away from my ear, "Will, what is the matter? What has he done? Why do they want him?"

I don't think, even then, that she realised what Humphrey had done. There was no point in making it clear to her. I have forgotten what I said to her but I know that I was as comforting as I could be. I promised that I would come to see her the next day and I told her to persuade Humphrey to go to the police if he got in touch with her. I think that I told her not to worry.

When I left the telephone box I had a moment of complete despair. Until then I had not realised how near Humphrey must have been to breaking point or that he was so entirely without courage. I had always thought of him as an exceptionally brave man; now it seemed that the standards by which I had judged him to be so were childish and illusory. Thinking like that left me with an odd feeling of emptiness.

I remember that I walked along the Embankment wondering where I had failed him.

I got to my club just before six o'clock. It was a fine evening, faintly cloudy in the sky, and cool. It was too late for tea and too early for dinner so I went into Park Lane and wandered aimlessly along the pavement. I turned down a side street into Shepherd Market, thinking what an unpleasantly self-conscious place it was and how much I disliked its snobbish little pretence of being a village in the middle of London. I went into the first pub I came to; it was quiet and hot and empty except for two men, one of them the man I least wished to meet.

I saw Piers as soon as I went in; if Piers had not seen me at the same time I think I would have gone away. But Piers nodded to me; the smile, in the heavy face, was bleak and unfriendly.

Piers had been talking to a man who moved away when I came

in and sat, unobtrusively, on a seat against the wall. He was a quite unremarkable man, it was only an odd sense of familiarity with him that made me notice him at all. He was dark-haired with a skin that was swarthy in an unhealthy way and he had narrow eyes under a low forehead that sloped sharply back to the line of the greased hair.

Piers offered me a drink and the barman brought whisky for us both. I drank mine quickly and ordered another. I wanted, childishly, to get the taste of the drink he had paid for out of my mouth. Piers stood facing me, one elbow on the bar. He was rolling his glass from one white hand to the other. There was a looking-glass on the wall behind him and I could see the back of his fat neck rolling over the collar of his coat. He looked intolerably smug.

I had eaten nothing since breakfast and the whisky released all my detestation of him and gave me a kind of stupid courage.

I said, "Piers, are you sure you did not know Rose?"

"Humphrey's little trollop? You must be slipping, William. I only met her once and I've already told you that."

He sounded over-emphatic. I said, "You know, I don't believe you."

Piers smiled, quite amiably. He said, "I don't see why you should insult me, William."

I muttered, "Don't you?" and felt, at once, like a rude, small boy. I said grudgingly, "I didn't mean to insult you. I only wanted to be sure. I thought you might have met her somewhere and forgotten."

He said, "Why should I forget, dear boy?" His voice was light and easy, his eyes as cold as winter stars.

I blundered on with an uneasy sense in the back of my mind that there was something that should be clear to me and was not. "It's even more important that we should find her now. Have you seen Humphrey?"

"Why should I have seen him?" he said.

"Don't you read the papers?" I asked. "He's run away. He was scared of the police."

He stared at me with amazement and disbelief. He said, "The

bloody fool. But he had nothing to do with the girl who was killed. Why should he run away?" He spoke with a kind of incredulous certainty.

I asked the barman for another whisky. I said, "But he had, you see. She was blackmailing him."

He said, "Dear God!" He was suddenly quite white; his face, for the moment, shocked into an expression of ordinary, human concern. It was the first time, I think, that I had seen him show any genuine and unaffected emotion. He said, in a whisper, "Why didn't he tell me?"

I began to realise that I had been drinking too quickly. The room was not quite steady and my stomach felt queasy. I shifted my position against the bar and my foot crunched on broken glass.

Piers said, to the barman, "Clumsy of me, Ron. Will you give me another?" The man poured him a fresh drink and came round the end of the counter to sweep up the broken glass.

Piers said, "When did this happen?"

I told him and he listened to me without comment, staring at the polished surface of the bar. When I had finished, he said, "This is almost the end for him, isn't it?" He sounded dispassionate, as if he were not really interested in Humphrey any more. It was almost as if he were washing his hands of him.

I said, "It isn't the end, by any means. It looks bad, of course. He saw the dead girl, with Rose, earlier in the evening. He's told the police that he saw her. He says he didn't see her again. I think he was afraid that the police wouldn't believe him. If we can find Rose we may be able to prove that he was telling the truth."

He said, "Dear boy, are you sure that she can be found? The police haven't found her. Are you cleverer than the police, William?"

He spoke in his ordinary, half-contemptuous fashion. He was playing with his glass, his small eyes glittered and he rocked gently on his feet. The brocade waistcoat was strained across his sagging belly.

I said, "The police are not infallible. And to them it must seem that he is guilty. He has acted as if he were guilty. We know he didn't do it. It gives us a kind of advantage. God knows it's all we've got."

I finished my whisky quickly. It helped me to face the awful knowledge that what I had just said was true.

Piers said, quite gently, "Are you sure about that? Are you a fool, William, or only very stubborn? You haven't been a very good judge of Humphrey up to now, have you? Wouldn't you be better employed in working out some kind of defence for him on the assumption that he did kill this girl, rather than chasing after the other one? Or do you see yourself as one of those engaging but unlikely gentlemen who appear in detective fiction? Really, William, aren't you just a little vain?"

I wanted to say, "But it's you, Piers, who are vain. Monstrously vain." I felt suddenly that this was something that was tremendously important although I wasn't sure why. I was aware of an, enormous anger. I wanted to hit his fat, red face and smash it into pulp.

I suppose I must have made some soft of aggressive movement because Piers stepped suddenly backwards as if to avoid a blow. Then I felt very ill. I left my drink standing on the bar counter and went to the lavatory. I was very sick and when I came back I felt sober and foolish. Piers had his back to the entrance and was talking again to the man with the unhealthy, dark skin. They were absorbed in each other. I went out of the pub.

The streets were crowded and the strolling couples had an air of summer leisure. The Park, across the road, was soft and green and sang with laughter,

I felt unbearably lonely. I stopped walking and stared into a shop window. A wax figure, draped in a pink nightdress, looked at me with a remote, sad air. My own reflection was imposed on the plate glass and it looked curiously, shadowy and transient. A sense of my own incompetence overwhelmed me; I felt a kind of panic.

I turned away from the window and called a taxi. I told the driver to go to The Odd Flamingo.

In the daylight the entrance to the club was drearier than I remembered it. The paint was peeling off the street door and the stairs to the basement were dirty. There was no one in the paybox at the top of the stairs and no one asked to see my membership card when I went into the downstairs room. The club was almost empty; the blank faces of the painted girls, perched on their bright, feathered bodies, made it seem trumpery and desolate.

The three men who made up the band were not playing but drinking at the bar. I bought a sandwich and a lager and sat down at one of the tables. The bread was stale and the beer warm but I began to feel better as soon as I had eaten.

Jennings had given me a photograph of Rose. I took it out of my pocket and looked at it. The great eyes stared at me, the mouth was soft and full and dreaming. I began to wonder if there was anything in the impulse that had brought me here; if she had come often, surely the barman would remember her? Or the band? They had their backs to me, presenting a solid wall of unapproachable black.

I had another beer and another stale sandwich. The man behind the counter was polishing glasses; the room was fuller now, but no one seemed to be buying drinks. The barman was a surly fellow; he listened with a kind of insolent inattention when I spoke to him and when I handed him the photograph he left a filthy fingermark on the edge of it.

He said, "No, I haven't seen her." His voice was final and sullen.

"Are you sure? She used to be a member?"

He watched me through his lashes. "Oh, did she?" he said. "If she was, mister, I'd have seen her. I'm telling you I haven't seen her." He was truculent about it. He gestured to the three men who made up the band. "Here, Stan," he said. "Seen this skirt before?"

The three men crowded round; they looked at the photograph and then, slyly, at me. One of them started to speak but the big one, the one the barman had called Stan, chipped in quickly and said, "I'd have noticed her all right if she'd been here." He sniggered loudly; the other two looked at him in what was somehow a furtive way and said nothing.

I took back the picture. I said, "I'm interested in another girl too. She . . ."

The barman said, "What's your business, mister? The white slaves?"

The band laughed loudly. I thought there was an uneasy note in their laughter. Most of the people in the room were watching us.

I think I was still a little drunk. I said, "The other girl was called Jasmine Castle. She was murdered."

The barman looked ugly. He said, "See here, mister. Are you trying to make trouble? Because if you are, we know what to do, see?"

The three men from the band had edged along the bar. The big one was standing very close to me.

I said, "I'm not trying to make trouble." I put the photograph back in my pocket and moved away. The men made room for me reluctantly.

Then I saw Kate. She was sitting by the wall. She was alone and her face was turned towards me. As I went over to her, she smiled and said, "Hullo, Willy. I thought you weren't going to speak to me."

I said, truthfully, "I didn't see you, Kate." I found, standing beside her, that I felt uneasy in her presence. I fancied, from the set expression of her lips, that she was uneasy too.

There was a short, embarrassed pause. Then she said, "Well, now you are here, aren't you going to buy me a drink?"

I said, "Of course. I'm sorry." I went to the bar and bought two whiskies and took them back to the table. I thought, looking at her, that she had grown very handsome with the years. The narrow, equine face that had prevented her from being a pretty girl gave her a grave charm in maturity. She had lost the air of restless excitement that had continually possessed her and acquired a kind of serenity. I realised that she must be nearly thirty and that she looked her age.

She gave me a small, amused smile. "Do I pass muster, Willy?"

I nodded. "I didn't mean to stare," I said.

She put her hand up to her ear and pulled gently at the lobe with her thumb and forefinger. It was a gesture I remembered. She said, "Do I look much older, Willy?"

I said gravely, "I think you are a great deal more attractive."

I think that pleased her. She smiled and said, "That's nice. But it wasn't what I asked. How are you, Willy? Are you married? Did you marry Celia?"

I shook my head. "No. She married Humphrey Stone."

She said, flushing, "I didn't know. I'm sorry." Her eyes shone. "That must have annoyed your mother, Willy. Though I always thought that it wasn't so much that she wanted you to marry Celia as that any woman would have been better than me."

The embarrassment I felt must have shown in my face because she added quickly, "That was clumsy of me. I'm sorry, Willy. I haven't changed, have I? Forgive me?"

I said, "There's nothing to forgive. You were quite right." And then I asked her what had been happening to her. It sounded, I think, rather stiff and conventional but I really wanted to know.

She said, "Very little, Willy. I'm not married.: I haven't a career. Only a job and a not very well paid one at that. In fact I've behaved in just the way you might have expected."

"Are you still painting?" I asked. When I had first known her she had been an art student; she had been noisy and opinionated and violent. I had thought that she painted rather well although I had known my judgment wasn't worth much. I had met her at a party and fallen in love with her almost at once. I had, for a short time, wanted desperately to marry her although she was not at all the sort of girl I had always thought I would marry. I had been, at that time, on the point of becoming engaged to Celia; we had known each other for years and I had thought myself in love with her although after I met Kate I knew that this was not true and never had been.

I had introduced Kate to my mother and it had been a failure from the beginning. My mother had disliked her and made little attempt to hide it. I think Kate had expected to be welcomed with kindness if not enthusiasm; when this did not happen she responded to my mother's frosty politeness with the truculence of a rude and angry child. Because she was hurt and because she had not yet learned to compromise she had flaunted the silly, unconventional ideas of the rackety set she belonged to, parading them proudly and defiantly as a peacock its tail until she had shocked my mother into indignant silence and departure. It was their only meeting; I did not attempt to arrange another. I was angry with Kate and, I think now, unsympathetic. We had the first of a long series of blazing rows in which I tried to make her behave as I wanted her to behave; how she would have to behave, I told her, if she became my wife. It wasn't until afterwards, when the final and most important trouble had blown up between us that it occurred to me that I might have been stiff and pompous and without understanding.

She said, "I haven't painted for years, Willy. I couldn't make my living that way and it didn't take long for me to realise that I hadn't the guts or the talent to go on. It was easier to get a job. I've had lots of jobs." She looked rueful and amused at the same time. "I'm not a very admirable character, Willy."

It wasn't said for effect; she had always had an honest belief in her own worthlessness.

She said abruptly, "Are you happy, Will?"

I said doubtfully, "I suppose so." It wasn't an easy question to answer. I had never thought much about it. I had been content but I thought that that was not what she had meant. I told her a little about the way I lived and found that it sounded dull.

She said, "At least you do something useful. I don't, you know. I've enjoyed myself, at least I think I have, but I haven't amounted to anything."

I said, "You're not old enough to be world-weary. And you used to talk like that when you were twenty, so it doesn't impress me over-much."

She said indignantly, "I'm not all that young now," and then she laughed at herself in the way that I remembered and said, "What were you doing at the bar?"

I said, "I was asking about a girl. Her name is Rose Blacker. You may have read about her in the papers."

She stared at me. "The girl who is missing? The one who was mixed up in the murder in Little Venice?"

I said, "She was a friend of the girl who was killed. No one knows where she is now." I hesitated for a moment and then I told her about Rose and about Humphrey. Her face was drained of colour; I thought that I had never seen anyone look so white.

At last she said, "But Willy, I've seen her. She used to come to the Flamingo. I recognised her when I saw her picture in the paper."

I said, incredulous, "But I asked the barman and the band. They said they had never seen her."

She said, "But that's not true. She came often. They must have seen her."

She spoke just loudly enough for the men to hear and the big one glanced angrily in her direction. She saw him and said, in a soft, hurried voice, "We can't talk here. Let's go out. Have you had dinner?"

She ran out of the room, ahead of me. It was almost as though something had suddenly frightened her. The light was on in the little box at the top of the narrow stair and the man who had sold me my membership card was seated inside. He drew back as I came level with the box, almost as though he didn't want to be seen, and made a great performance of lighting a cigarette.

I recognised him now without difficulty. He was the man who had been in the pub at Shepherd's Market. The unremarkable man with the greasy hair. The man who had been talking to Piers.

Kate took me to a restaurant that she knew. It was small and cheap but the food was good and the tablecloths were clean. The woman who ran the place greeted Kate as if she knew her well; she stood by our table for a while and talked. She asked Kate whether she was quite better now and Kate said yes, quite better, as though she did not want to talk about herself. When the woman had gone away I asked her if she had been ill and she flushed and said, almost curtly, that she had been in hospital for a little while, that was all.

She offered no further explanation and, looking at her in the cruel light of the café, I thought that she looked tired and much too thin. I wondered if she ate enough; she played with her food as if she did not really want it and was only eating to be sociable. I wondered how much she earned and, sentimentally, if there was anyone to see that she looked after herself. Her parents had been already dead when I had first known her and she had never mentioned any other relatives. I remember that it had surprised me, lapped around as I was by family, that she should apparently have none.

We talked, while we ate, but not of Rose. It was almost as though Kate did not want to talk about her. I found, a little to my surprise, I think, that we had a great deal to talk about. So much, in fact, that by the time we were drinking coffee I felt as if it were impossible that I had not seen her for so long a time. It was the sort of restaurant we had always gone to together; I had been a captain in the gunners when we had first met and quite able to afford something better, but Kate had affected to despise the better places.

In the end I said directly, "Kate, will you tell me about Rose?"

She said with some slight nervousness, "You know, I may be hopelessly wrong. Will you show me the photograph?"

I gave it to her. She looked at it for a moment and then she nodded. "I'm quite sure that is the girl," she said.

She lit a cigarette and stared at the tablecloth. She told me a little of what she knew. I thought, at the time, that she had told me everything.

She had first seen Rose one evening in the late spring. She had come into the Flamingo with a crowd of young men and one other girl. The men were noisy and a little drunk, they wore thickly padded suits and they carried flashy cigarette cases. The other girl was pretty and vivacious and Kate had thought her rather ordinary.

Rose, on the other hand, was far from ordinary and, in those surroundings, completely unexpected. Kate said, with a sincerity that prevented her words from sounding cheap and sentimental, that the girl had been as out of place in the Flamingo as a country flower in a town alley.

She said; "I don't know how to explain it. It wasn't just that she was obviously young and exceptionally lovely to look at, although that would have been impressive enough. She looked so extraordinarily *innocent*, Willy. It was startling and in an odd sort of way almost horrifying."

The party sat at the biggest table in the club and bought a good many drinks. The boys paid for everything with notes. Kate had been seated near to their table and had heard a great deal of what was said. None of it she remembered; there had been a lot of pointless innuendo, nudging and sudden laughter. Rose had said very little except, "I don't mind," when she was offered a drink. She laughed when the others did but a little after them, as if she did not know what she was laughing at. Later in the evening one of the men sat next to her. He put his arm round her shoulders and fondled her. Rose did not attempt to move away; she sat still, like a little doll, without any expression on her face at all. By the time that Kate left the club Rose was leaning her head against the man's shoulder, hiccuping a little, and her eyes were closed.

Kate said, "The man I was with said . . ." She stopped and suddenly blushed as if she did not want to tell me what he had said.

I said, "Go on," and she looked at me oddly and warily as if she wasn't sure what to say next. Then she talked more slowly and with a new caution. I thought that she was afraid of saying too much. I wondered why. I remember that I was feeling sick at the thought of Rose in The Odd Flamingo.

Kate said that she went to the club fairly frequently. I did not ask her why she went although I wondered why. I thought her too adult for that kind of place; it did not occur to me then that she might be lonely, and that when you are lonely any place where you are known is better than no place at all.

Rose had been to the club quite often, usually with the same group of young men, sometimes with only one of them. She always seemed quite ludicrously out of place, although after the first time she seemed more at ease and laughed and talked quite happily.

I said, "What about her friends? The men she came with. Would you recognise them again?"

She said doubtfully, "I expect I would. But they were all very ordinary. There wasn't anything about them to remember."

I said, "If she went there so often, why on earth didn't the barman recognise her photograph?"

She didn't look at me. She said, "I don't know. Perhaps he didn't want to be mixed up in anything. They live in an odd sort of world, Willy." She looked at me almost shyly.

I said, "It isn't a very pleasant kind of world, is it?"

She said, "I suppose not." Her eyes were bright and hurt. She said, trying to laugh, "It's my kind of world, you know."

I hadn't meant to hurt her. I said, "I'm sorry. I'm a fool." Then I said, "Is there anyone else who might have known Rose? It would be useful to have another witness if we are to go to the police."

She said, "The police?" in a startled way as if she had not thought of them as being concerned in the matter at all.

I said, "Of course we shall have to go to the police." She said reluctantly, "I suppose so." She piled her cigarette ash into a little heap and knocked it down again. "We could go and see Carl," she said.

On the way she said, "Carl was with me the night that I met you in the Flamingo. Remember? The man who wouldn't let go of me. He's not so bad, really. He's a queer, but he's kind. He's beastly when he gets drunk but he's always very sorry about it afterwards."

She spoke as if she had a real affection for him.

Carl was at home. When he opened the door I saw that he was dressed in a bright robe of scarlet silk that swept from his little shoulders to his tiny feet. He was almost grotesquely small, his brown face was little and sharp like a monkey's. He greeted us in a high, thin voice, waving his hands wildly in welcome.

"Lovely of you to come," he said. "I was perfectly *wretched* as one is when one has decided to spend the evening at home and do a great many dull domestic things. Delightful as a prospect but quite incredibly dreary in fact. I'll make you some coffee—I make *perfect* coffee, don't I, Kate?"

It was very ordinary coffee, I thought, and almost cold because

Carl insisted on filtering it through metal containers in the French way. But Carl was very proud of it; he was pleased with himself. He talked a great deal in his cheeping, sexless voice. The room was littered with small china figures. He brought them to me, one by one, to be admired and exclaimed over. He was like a child showing his toys. When he touched my hand my flesh crawled with a disgust that I could not control. I tried to hide it.

After a while he stopped talking for long enough for Kate to explain why we had come. He listened to her intently, his bright, intelligent eyes not moving from her face.

He pouted, "And I thought you had come to see *me*. I was so dull and that dreadful Rowley had gone out and left me all alone. We'd had a quarrel you see, and he'd gone out to *punish* me." He sounded petulant. "And after all you only wanted to see me so that you could find out some dreadfully sordid *facts*. Such a blow. Never mind—give me the picture and I'll tell you if I know her."

I gave him the photograph and he gloated over it.

"Such eyes, what a stupid little beauty. Of course I've seen her. How very stupid of the people at the Flamingo not to know. She was there quite often. Such a lovely change from the dreary, dreary people—I always thought her quite exquisite, almost as lovely as my Dresden figurines. Only not quite so lovely, of course, because she was alive. There's nothing like animation for *ruining* beauty like this. It should always be calm, perfectly calm and still."

He clasped his delicate hands together in a kind of rapture. Under the tightly drawn skin the bones of his hands looked like birds' bones. My flesh began to crawl again as I looked at him. I glanced at Kate and she was watching Carl with a kind of amused, maternal fondness.

I said, "Do you know the men she was with at the club?"

"Oh yes," he said. "Not by name, you know, except one. The one she was with most often. Rowley and I used to call him 'the wide boy.' Such a pretty term. He was the perfect little spiv. That isn't anything uncommon at the Flamingo, of course. There isn't anything *villainous* about any of them, they're very mild little spivs. The kind who used to sell nylons in Oxford Street—you can get nylons now, so I expect they are selling something \ else. Steel, perhaps. This one wore the most delicious socks. He had one *quite* original pair and I begged him to tell me where he'd bought them so that I could buy a pair for Rowley's birthday, but he was dreadfully rude and refused to tell me.

"Everyone used to call him Jimmie. I don't remember what they called your girl. They didn't appreciate her, of course. I tried to talk to her one evening and this Jimmie fellow came up to me and said some very *common* things. He said that he would `flatten my face for me.'"

Carl looked pained and gestured with his tiny hands. "I ask you, was that kind? When all I had done was to tell his girl that she was like some precious, rare orchid? It was an unpleasant little scene and not at all worth while, because the girl hadn't appreciated the lovely things I'd said to her. She looked at me all the time with her beautiful mouth ever so slightly open as if she couldn't breathe properly through her nose. If these lovely creatures *have* to be alive, then they ought to have some character. Jimmie's other girl had plenty. I think he must have found your Rose a little dim after Jasmine."

I said "Jasmine?" and Carl looked at me carefully as if he were suddenly on his guard.

He said, "You didn't know her too?"

"No," I said. "I didn't know her." I hoped my face wasn't giving too much away.

Carl went on, prattling happily like a child at a treat. "She wasn't as beautiful as Rose, but then she had a thought or two in her pretty head and thought always takes away from beauty. She looked like a peach, all yellow and gold and velvety. I remember that I said so to Rowley and he was quite ridiculously jealous." He giggled archly and happily. "She was always very gay and wild and imperious—she treated us all as if she were a queen and we were her subjects. Sometimes, when she was drunk, I used to call her the changeling."

His voice was warm as though he had been fond of Jasmine. He considered for a moment with his head on one side, looking like an old, old child who had dressed up in his mother's house-coat. The high collar stood up stiffly; round his small, brown face. "I like that word," he said. "It's a prettier one than delinquent."

"What do you mean?" I said.

He looked evasive. "Well, she was, wasn't she? The poor child?"

"Did you know she was dead?" I said.

The monkey face jerked sharply towards me and I was sure that the sudden look of horror and surprise was genuine.

He said. "But how sad. How terrible. Poor, pretty child."

"She was murdered," I said and to my intense surprise and embarrassment Carl bowed his head and made the sign of the cross on his silken chest. It was not entirely theatre. He said, "God rest her soul," and I was sure he meant it. There were tears in the sharp little eyes.

I told him then, briefly and guardedly, why it was important that I should find Rose. "Where does this Jimmie live?" I said. "Where could I find him?"

Carl gave me a sideways look. "You aren't thinking that he killed the poor girl, are you? He's not at all that sort of boy. He's small fry, the kind that doesn't kill. I don't know where he lives. We weren't on speaking terms."

I said, "How long is it since you first saw Rose at the club?"

He wrinkled up his little nose. "I don't know. Facts aren't in my line. It's only recently, I think. In the last six months or so. I practically *live* there, you see. It's so full of human oddity. I get beautifully drunk there and when I'm drunk my head gets as clear as crystal. It's a delightful sensation." He was looking at me as he spoke and I wondered if he drugged. His eyes looked odd and his whole face had a curiously bright look.

I said, "How does the place pay? You go there often, don't you? No one seems to buy many drinks and they aren't particularly expensive."

His mouth twitched. "Are you thinking of a gambling hell? It's not that. None of these foolish little places pay. They run for a year or so and then they go bankrupt and start up under another name."

I did not say that this place had not gone bankrupt, that it had been in existence, to my knowledge, for at least twelve years. I said instead, "Don't you know anyone who could tell me more about Jimmie?"

He said, "Why, any of the other little spivs would know. But if the poor girl has been killed I should think they would be avoiding the Flamingo for a while just in case the police should want to talk to them. They are all a little shy of attracting attention from that quarter. Not that the police are showing much interest in the club at the moment. They aren't lucky, like you. They haven't me as a source of information."

He chuckled, peeping at me shyly from the shelter of his bright collar. Then he said, "There is one person who might know. Though one would think you had already asked him. Piers Stone. He is your friend's half-brother, isn't he?"

I said, "But how would he know? He didn't go to the place." I felt a kind of chill as if the summer's night had suddenly grown cold.

Carl said softly, "Now I wonder why he told you that?" His voice was patiently enquiring. "He isn't what you might call a frequent visitor, but he is a member. And I thought that he knew our Jimmie."

I said, "And Rose? Did he know her too?"

Carl frowned, he looked unhappy as though he was aware, suddenly, that he had said more than he had meant to say. He said, delicately, "He may have done. One can never tell." He looked at the clock on the mantelpiece. He was uneasy, his hands twitched and he did not look at either of us. "Just *look* at the time," he said. "Beddy-byes for little Carl. I had been promising myself some beauty sleep to-night."

It wasn't very late but the dismissal was clear. I looked at Kate. She was sitting on the floor with her hands clasped round her knees.

Her face was white and stiff with shock and fear.

Chapter Eight

Carl saw us out of the flat, twittering brightly about nothing. His bird's eyes flickered from Kate to me in a way that made him look furtive and alarmed. In the cruel light of the naked bulb on the landing outside the flat his little face looked old and sad and his brilliant coat seemed a pathetically tawdry piece of flamboyance.

In the street Kate walked beside me with the width of the pavement between us. There was a new and sudden constraint between us; the earlier, comforting sense of friendship had gone. When she spoke at last there was a forced, false note in her voice as though she were uncertain how I would take what she was going to say.

"You know, I shouldn't pay too much attention to Carl. He's a dear, and I'm fond of him, but he's not always truthful. And he likes to make mischief."

She turned towards me for the first time since we had left the fiat and gave me a bright, artificial smile.

I said, "Do you mean that he was lying when he said that Piers was a member of the club?"

She hesitated. "No. It isn't that. He suggested, didn't he, that Piers might be mixed up in this business? He couldn't—I mean he doesn't know. He only said it because he hates Piers. Carl is the sort of person no one ever trusts. No one ever tells him anything."

I said, "Kate, what is the matter? Are you afraid?"

She said, "Most people are afraid." Her voice was flat and final as if she didn't want to say any more. She went on, "Please, Willy, don't pry. It doesn't concern you."

I said, bewildered, "I don't know what you're talking about. I don't want to pry."

She peered at me in the gloom and then she laughed and it sounded high and foolish in the soft night. She touched my hand lightly and said, "I've upset you, and for nothing. When Carl started to talk about Piers I was afraid he was going to tell you something I didn't want you to know. Something there is no need for you to know."

I took her hand and said, "I'm sorry, Kate. But if he was a member of this club why should he say that he never went there? Why should he bother to lie about it?"

Her voice was stiff and unnatural. "Perhaps he was too vain to tell you the truth. It isn't a very smart sort of place, is it? Besides, it's almost true. He doesn't go there very often."

I said, "Did he know this Jimmie?"

The hand I was holding trembled a little as she pulled it away. She said, "Perhaps. I don't know." Suddenly there was hysteria in her voice. "Don't ask me, Willy. It's not my business. I won't be mixed up in it."

I said, "Kate, what on earth is the matter? What have I done?"

She had turned her face away from me and she was standing quite still. She shook her head violently. I thought that she was near to tears and it unnerved me. I said gently, "If I could help you, can't you tell me?"

Her shoulders heaved and she began to cry in a desperate, silent way. The tears ran down her face and she made no attempt to wipe them away.

I said, unhappily, "I don't want to dig into something that you want to keep private. But I must find Rose. It isn't just because of Humphrey, though God knows that's important enough." I nearly said that she seemed the only worth-while person in the whole, sordid business, that if it weren't for her, I wouldn't be dirtying my hands. But I was afraid that Kate would laugh at me for a sentimental fool.

She said, almost with anger, "Willy, I can't help you, I swear I can't. Do you want to humiliate me beyond bearing?"

She sounded in agony. I felt foolish and helpless and suddenly rather moved. I took her in my arms and for a moment she stayed there with her head on my shoulder. I could feel her whole body shaking. Then she moved away and looked up into my face and said, "Willy, I swear that I know nothing that would help you to find Rose. It's entirely a personal matter. You know, I could use a drink."

She had put aside her emotion completely; her control made me feel useless and shut out because I would have liked to have been able to help her.

We went to a pub where there were wooden tables and striped umbrellas set out on the pavement. The night was cool. Across the road was the park and the couples walking among the trees. I felt a kind of peace; I think I would have been almost happy if Kate had not begun to laugh and talk with a strained and artificial gaiety, reminding me that we were strangers and wary of each other.

Kate drank a great deal and it quietened her. Her eyes began to look glazed and sleepy.

She said, "Willy, you're very fond of Humphrey, aren't you?"

I said, "Yes. I suppose he is my best and oldest friend." I wondered why she should voluntarily open a subject that had seemed distasteful to her.

"And you do believe that he didn't kill this girl? That he hasn't got it in him?"

I said, "I have to believe that he couldn't do it."

She said, with surprising venom, "You see, if it were Piers, I shouldn't find it surprising at all. He's capable of anything."

Her face had altered so that I thought that if I were to meet her now, not expecting to see her, I would not recognise her. Hatred is one of the most disfiguring of emotions.

I said, as gently as I could, "Kate, what has he done to you?"

She looked at me, faintly startled, as if for a moment she had forgotten that I was there. Then she said, "To me? Nothing much. Any harm that was done I did myself. It's what he is."

She hesitated, and then, in a voice that was slightly drunk and entirely solemn, she said, "I think he is the Anti-Christ."

Her mouth twitched and she smiled in a white, exhausted fashion.

"Sorry, Will. Boozer's hysterics. I think I'd better go home before I embarrass you."

On the way home, first in the taxi and later, walking along the embankment by the river because she said that she did not want to go home straightaway, I tried to find out why she had said what she did. It was without any success; she had sobered quickly and would not be drawn.

After I had kissed her good-night she looked up into my face and said, "Willy, I shouldn't cross swords with Piers. It won't help you and he's a bad person to be your enemy. He is greedy and quite extraordinarily vain. It makes him dangerous, I think."

There was concern on her face and in her voice. Her eyes shone in the lamplight; she had very beautiful eyes. I was suddenly quite painfully aware of how much I had loved her and of how wilfully and stupidly I had thrown it away. I was not in love with her now; there was only regret and an intolerable sense of waste.

I said, "Kate, am I to see you again?"

She smiled at me warmly and with casual affection. "If you want to, Willy," she said. The politeness in her voice hurt me more than if she had said she did not want to see me again although I knew that I had no right to ask anything of her any more.

As I left her the bitterness and hatred that I had felt for Piers was as clear and newly-minted as the day that he had told me that Kate had been, and still was, his mistress. I remembered the smile on his face and the amusement in his eyes and if he had been there I think I would have killed him.

When I got to my club the porter said that there was someone waiting for me in the lounge. He sounded a little aggrieved about it as if he thought it was too late for respectable visitors.

I don't know whom I had expected to see but it wasn't Jennings. He was sitting there patiently, upright in a leather chair, his feet planted primly together. He got up as I came in and said, "Good-evening, Mr. Hunt."

He looked shabby and tidy and tired.

I was suddenly and happily sure about what he had come to

tell me. I said, "Have you found Rose?" I felt, for a moment, ridiculously light-hearted as if nothing else mattered at all.

Then he shook his head and looked at me in a surprised sort of way.

"I'm afraid not," he said, and his face fell into lines of worry and unhappiness. "We've found no trace of her," he said.

I asked him what had been done and he told me. It all sounded very cold and official and unhelpful. I asked him about The Odd Flamingo and he said yes, the police knew that she used to go there. He didn't sound very interested; he listened with his good ear carefully inclined towards me when I told him what I had learned from Carl. He didn't seem to be particularly impressed and I didn't blame him. It sounded, in the re-telling, inconclusive and not very convincing.

I began to realise that Jennings thought her dead; he had spoken of her in the past tense. He told me, in the end, that they had decided to drain part of the canal.

I felt abominably sick. I said, "But she can't be dead," and he looked at me sadly with his nice, anxious eyes and said, "I hope you're right, Mr. Hunt. I hope very much that you are right."

I felt in need of a drink and I asked Jennings if he would join me. He hesitated and said that he wasn't, strictly speaking, on duty, and that he would like a whisky. He was a trifle pompous about it as though it was an event for him to have a drink at all.

While we were waiting for the drinks he talked about the weather. He was very polite all the time and very unassuming.

Then he told me something about The Odd Flamingo that did not surprise me but rather confirmed a suspicion in my own mind.

He said, "That club. The Odd Flamingo. We've had our eye on it for some time. We watch all these places, of course, and there may be nothing in it. Some of the members are petty criminals—mostly small thieves and delinquents. There's no evidence to show the place is up to anything illegal, you understand, but there have been cases recently when we have interviewed a man and found that he's spent the evening he's being questioned about at the club. Plenty of people to vouch for him and all that sort of thing. It may be quite genuine, of course, but it's happened rather too often recently."

I wondered what it was all leading up to; I thought it unlikely that he was just making general conversation.

Then he looked at the golden liquid in his glass. "It seems an odd sort of place for a man like Mr. Stone," he said.

I said, "You can't be accused because of the company you keep. Or is it a new law?"

He said, "We aren't accusing Mr. Stone of anything." He smiled at me over his glass and I felt that I had been put in the wrong. His eyes were very bright. I knew why he had come to see me.

I said, "I don't know where Humphrey is. I wish to God I did."

He looked carefully away from me. He said, unconvincingly, "I am sure that if you did know, Mr. Hunt, you would persuade him to come to see us. If he has done nothing, then he has nothing to be afraid of, has he? But it is unfortunate that he has gone away. It makes it difficult for us to think him entirely innocent."

He smiled at me again and finished his drink. I was sure that he had no personal doubt about Humphrey's' guilt but for the moment that didn't worry me so much as the realisation that he believed that I knew where to find him.

It made me realise, much later, when Jennings had gone and I lay awake in my narrow bed, that I did, in fact, know where Humphrey might be.

I don't think I slept at all. I know that I heard every hour strike. I was facing, I think, for the first time, the fact that Rose might be dead. Until this evening it had seemed an academic possibility merely; now, remembering Jennings's calm, precise voice speaking of her in the past tense, I knew a kind of terror and despair that I had never known before. She must be alive. I found myself saying so, out aloud and defiantly to the still night. Because if she were dead, then the whole thing was hopeless and useless and I wanted no more part in it.

Then the light came and the sound of the first, sleepy birds. I got up and asked the night porter for my bill and got the car out of the garage.

It was a lovely morning, clean and cool with a slight sting in the air that suggested that the long heat was over and it was nearly autumn. I opened the roof of the car and drove fast along the clear roads until I began to feel a little less like a man in a nightmare.

I got home at about six o'clock. The house was silent and the blinds at my mother's window were drawn. I bathed and made myself breakfast and ate it in the quiet, cool kitchen.

I went into the garden for a little while and then I drove down to the School. Celia came to the door and opened it a foot or so and peered out at me, blinking in the light. She wore a crumpled cotton dress and she looked hopelessly tired.

I went into the hall and she closed the door quickly, leaning against it as if she were barring out the world.

She said, "Will, Humphrey rang up last night."

I said, "Where is he? Did you tell him to go to the police?"

She nodded. "He wouldn't listen to me. He wouldn't say where he was. Just that he was all right and I was to try not to worry too much. It was a local call and he must have been in a box because I heard him press Button A. If he'd been far away the call would have gone through the exchange."

Her voice was husky and controlled. She ran her hand through her hair. "Would you like some coffee, Will? I want some. I haven't had any breakfast."

We went into the kitchen. She said, "The police came last night just after I'd spoken to Humphrey. I was afraid, for a bit, that they'd heard me talking on the telephone. They asked me lots of questions about where he might be. What will happen if they find him, Will?"

She was wandering wretchedly about the kitchen, a kettle in her hand. I took it from her and put it on the stove and lit the gas. She leant wearily against the table looking both distracted and spent.

I said, "I don't know. It looks bad for him, of course. But I don't think they can have much of a case against him until they find

Rose. And I hope that when she turns up they won't have a case at all. I want to try and find her."

She said quietly, "Unless we find her there isn't much hope, is there? But if the police haven't found her, how can we?"

I said, "The police think she is dead'. I think she is alive. I'm going to find her."

As I said it I thought that it sounded a stupid piece of bravado. She did not answer. I made the coffee and put the milk in a saucepan to heat. All the time there was silence except for the small, domestic sounds. When I looked at her, finally, I saw that her prominent blue eyes were cold.

She said, "Will, how can you? You don't know how to set about that sort of thing."

I said, "I know. I know all that." I poured the milk carefully out of the saucepan into a blue jug. It seemed to help to concentrate on little things.

I said, "I think I've made a start. I'm not being entirely foolish."

I tried, for her sake, to sound sure of myself and cheerful and I think I succeeded. She managed to smile at me and, in spite of her pallor and the muddy circles under her eyes, she looked a little less wan.

She said, "Will, there is one thing I don't understand. If the baby wasn't Humphrey's, why did she come to me and pretend that it was? What reason could she have? It was a dangerous thing to do, wasn't it? It was blackmail."

I realised then that I hadn't thought about that part of it for a long time. Perhaps because I hadn't wanted to.

I said, "She may have thought that Humphrey was more likely to help her. She may have been rather desperate, you see. It may have seemed, to her, that he was comparatively rich and becuse of his job he wouldn't want to be mixed up in that kind of scandal."

I nearly added that it might, after all, be Humphrey's child. That I had been almost quite sure, at the time, that she was speaking the truth. But I think that to have said so just then would have been an unnecessary unkindness.

I poured out the coffee and Celia sat on the kitchen table and drank it, curling her hands round the cup as though she were cold.

She said suddenly, "Will, Humphrey will lose his job, won't he? Even if they don't arrest him? I've been thinking about that all night. We shall have to leave this house. I don't know where we shall go. Probably one of those horrid, poky houses along the by-pass. I don't know how I shall bear it—leaving this lovely, lovely house." Her face looked small and pinched. "Don't be angry with me, Will. I know it sounds silly and shallow and beside what may happen to Humphrey it isn't important at all. Only thinking about Humphrey is like standing on the edge of a pit that you daren't look into because you know there is something dreadful there. So I've been thinking about the house instead and worrying about where we shall go and what we shall do. I've lived here all my life—first with Daddy and then with Humphrey. I can't imagine living anywhere else."

She looked so woebegone that my heart was stung with pity for her.

I said, "Dear, don't worry about that. Not yet. It may be all right, you may not have to go."

I knew that it was not true and she knew it too, but she gave me a thin, grateful smile. Then she said, "Will, do you believe that Humphrey killed that girl?"

It was a question I had not yet faced in my own mind because I had not dared to do so. That Celia should have been able to face it and put it into words made me despise myself.

I said, "My dear, how can I possibly know? I don't think he was capable of that, whatever else he may have done."

The tightness of her face relaxed and she began to cry. I comforted her as well as I could and tried to talk of other things. I did my best to sound more hopeful than I felt—I thought, when I left, that she looked a little better. There was more colour in her face and she smiled at me without effort. She stood in the doorway and watched me go, her legs bare and thin as rods beneath her cotton skirt.

I went to the office and worked for most of the day. It wasn't easy but I had to get through the day somehow.

I had dinner at home and went out in the early dark. I drove out of the town towards the low hills and the wooded ridge that ran across country, level with the sea. The land was populous, stockbrokers' country, but the ridge had been very little built on. There was no good road and most of it belonged to the small local squire who had been an old man when I was young and did nothing with his land except let the shooting and keep a few sheep. When we had been boys the ridge had been a paradise for us and the place of endless games. Humphrey used to stay with me during our holidays from school and it was one summer vacation that we had found the hide-out. I hadn't been there for years and I wasn't at all sure that I could find it again.

I left the car in a side-lane, hidden from the main road by the thick, summer hedges. I climbed towards the ridge, keeping in the shelter of the ditches that bordered the fields. The wheat grew high, almost to my shoulder, and the heavy ears cracked in the wind.

The climb was steeper than I remembered; when I got to the top it was nearly dark and the trees were black against a sky of deepest violet. I wondered if I would be able to find the mound from which you could see the sea. The hide-out was near it, a patch of gorse bushes below a rough, chalk track.

I walked along the ridge for perhaps half-an-hour before I found the place. I had begun to think that I would never find it when I stumbled up on to the naked promontory of chalky earth and in the distance, miles away, there was a moving light that might have been a ship.

Standing alone on the mound I had a sudden moment of unease. There was a little, moaning wind in the tree tops and the whole empty country seemed suddenly full of the kind of noises that you hear when you are alone in the dark and fearful.

I saw the track and the gorse bushes at my feet and with memory rather than sight I found the narrow cut that led steeply down between them to the earthwork that had been hidden by their roots. I tore my trousers on the grasping branches of the gorse and the spiky stems whipped across my face with sudden pain. At the bottom of the cut I was in what was almost a hole in the ground; it was a forgotten earthwork of some kind and the gorse had grown all around it and met over the top, shutting out the sky.

It was smelly and damp. I called Humphrey's name and lit a match. The match spurted and blew out. I dropped the match box and as I bent to pick it up he said, "Hullo, Will."

He was half way up the side of the earthwork, crouching in the gorse. The match flared up brightly and I saw him clearly, his knees drawn up against the side of the hole, his arms outstretched and clinging on to the gorse. He looked filthy; the whites of his eyes were a dirty yellow colour and bloodshot.

He said, "I wondered if you would come," and dropped on to the ground beside me. He was breathing heavily and he smelt appallingly of sweat and dirt and fear.

I said, my voice loud with relief, "Well, you've made a pretty mess for yourself, haven't you? How d'you think I'm going to get you out of it now?"

He said, "Shut up, for God's sake. Do you want to bring them about my ears?"

The match went out and I could see nothing of him except a patch of lighter darkness which was his flaxen head.

I said, "No one saw me come. I swear it." I gave him a cigarette and he lit it thankfully. We crouched on the damp floor of the hole and talked in whispers. I said to him all the things I had planned to say. I pleaded with him, bullied him and encouraged him. And all the time he stayed as still as stone, a sullen, angry stranger, out of my reach. I could only guess at the depth of his terror; he had all the blind, irrational panic of the hunted man, nothing mattered to him any longer except that he should not be caught. I asked, to shock him into reason, whether he had killed Jasmine Castle. He denied it dully and without feeling, as if it were not important.

I told him that I was looking for Rose. I began to ask him questions, small, practical things. He was quite logical and clear when he answered me.

I said, "Did you know that Piers was a member of The Odd

Flamingo? He told me that he never went there. That it wasn't his sort of place."

Humphrey said, "He's always posing, you know. Maybe he thought it wasn't grand enough. He has a ridiculously inflated sense of dignity."

I said, "The police think there is something fishy about the place. Did you notice anything?"

My eyes were used to the darkness now and I saw him grin. "I was usually tight," he said. "It isn't the sort of place to contemplate sober."

I asked him if he had ever met anyone called Jimmie and he was doubtful. "I don't think so. There were any number of youngsters I knew by their christian names, but I don't remember a Jimmie. There was a James. Piers called him James, anyway. That's his way. He likes to be formal. He thinks it makes him sound like a nice old Edwardian gent. This boy was about twenty. Would he be the one?"

I said, "I don't know. Tell me about him."

Humphrey had only seen him once. The boy had lint-white hair and he wore a cheap, smart suit, very broad across the shoulders and very tight round the hips. He carried what seemed to be a great deal of money in an expensive pigskin case. He had been on his own on the evening that Humphrey had met him with Piers and it seemed, though Humphrey could not be sure about it, that Piers had met him before.

He said, "They seemed pretty matey. James seemed to think a great deal of Piers. He listened to him as if he were listening to God Almighty. It seemed a bit out of character in a boy like that. Piers lapped it up. He likes adulation, you know. You'd never think it was all that important to him, would you? That he should be admired, I mean."

I asked, "Do you remember what they talked about?"

"I don't think I do. I wasn't very interested, honestly. He wasn't a particularly pleasant young man."

I said slowly, "Humphrey, have you any idea how Piers makes a living?"

Humphrey shifted his position on the damp bottom of the earthwork. "God, I don't know. I never enquire. You know his mother left him a packet when he was twenty-one? He spent it all in a couple of years. I think it's probably true what he says—he lives on horse-racing. He's surprisingly adept at it. I don't expect he pays income tax or anything silly like that."

I said, "What was his interest in this boy?"

"I don't know. He likes to be admired and he was getting it in full measure from this kid. You know his usual line of patter? Always agin the government and saying how stupid it is to pay attention to law and order when you can get on so much better without it. I don't know that he'd ever do anything illegal himself—apart from the small matter of not paying his taxes—but he likes to see other people misbehaving themselves." He laughed softly. "I must say he makes it sound practically a moral duty."

I said, "You mean he goes round inciting people to break the law?"

Humphrey said, "Leave him alone, Will. He's a dishonest bastard, but I love him." His manner had become, while we were talking, almost light and easy as though we were sitting in the drawing-room at the School and not crouching, like rabbits, on the floor of the burrow.

Now, suddenly, the sound of fear was back in his voice. He said, "I rang him up last night. After I'd spoken to Celia. I rang from a box on the Folkestone Road. I was terrified all the time. There were a lot of cars going by and the headlights seemed to pick me out. I thought he'd be able to help, you see. He knows a lot of shady people I thought he'd be able to tell me where to go. But he didn't, want to talk to me. He said he couldn't help, that it was too dangerous. He said the best thing I could do was to stay out of the way for as long as I could. It was almost as though he wanted to be rid of me."

He sounded helpless and surprised. I said, "God damn him to hell," a righteous and ridiculous anger filled me. I think I was surprised, too. I had thought that Piers's affection for Humphrey was the only genuine thing about him.

There was a silence that hung heavily and awkwardly between us. Then Humphrey said, "Will, have you got any money? I may need it. I took some food from the house."

I gave him all I had in my wallet and he, took it with too much gratitude so that I felt a kind of revulsion. I had no love for him any more, only a forced and unhappy pity.

There was nothing else that I could do for him. I think I wished him luck and told him that if there was anything I could do that he was to get in touch with me. We were both embarrassed and suddenly conventional. I remember that we shook hands with great and absurd solemnity.

And then I went away and left him in his rat-hole.

Chapter Nine

I went to the office in the morning and tidied up my work as well as I could. After lunch I drove to London; it was still very hot and there was little traffic on the roads, so that I reached the West End in a shorter time than usual. In Maida Vale the streets slept in the sun; the roar of buses on the main road sounded muted and benign.

The blinds in the flat were drawn. When Piers opened the door he looked sluggish and the contours of his face were sagging as if he had been asleep.

He said, "It's you, is it? What do you want?"

His head, on the thick neck, was thrust forward. He stared at me with sleepy eyes. He looked like an old, belligerent rhinoceros.

I said, "Piers, I want to talk to you." Then as soon as I had spoken, I was afraid. I didn't know why. I only knew that fear had come upon me without warning and that my mouth was dry.

Piers stood aside. "You had better come in," he said.

The flat was untidy and unkempt. The air smelt sweaty and stale. The blue cat snarled at me, indolent on his silken cushion. Piers lay down on the sofa before the darkened window, his head in shadow. He was half-dressed, his paunch hung loosely over the top of his trousers. He looked seedy and middle-aged. His voice had none of its usual suavity, it was grumpy and bad-tempered. He hated to be caught at a disadvantage.

He said, with his eyes shut, "Well, William? Say what you have to say and go."

All the time I had been driving to London I had rehearsed what I was going to say to Piers and now the words had gone from my mind. There only remained a kind of pointless anger.

At last I said, and the words sounded awkward and stumbling, "I want to ask about a young man you knew at The Odd Flamingo. A young man called James."

Piers sat upright on the sofa. He said, "How very extraordinary you are, William. Why should I know anything about your young man?"

His face was not bad-tempered now, but bland and unrevealing.

I said, "I know you used to go to the club although you told me you did not. I don't know why you should lie about it—your pretensions to grandeur do not concern me. But I am interested in James. It was only you who called him James, wasn't it? Everyone else called him Jimmie."

Piers stared at me, his eyes bright and fixed. Then he said, "It is inconceivable to me, dear boy, why you should interest yourself in this young man. As for your explanation of why I did not want to identify myself with the club, it is typical of you. But it is not your business; Is that understood?"

His voice was cold. He was in control of himself.

I said, "I want to know Jimmie's other name and where I can find him."

Piers laughed. "Do you think that I know the name and address of every young scoundrel I speak to? William, I think you must be a little mad."

He made a contemptuous gesture with his white hands and lifted his legs back on to the sofa and closed his eyes.

My hands were shaking and I pushed them into my trousers pockets to keep them still. I said, "Piers, this is important. Rose used to go to The Odd Flamingo with a boy called Jimmie. I want to find him and her. I want to help Humphrey. Don't you?"

He got up heavily from the sofa and lumbered across the room. He took a cigarette from a silver box and lit it.

He said, "I'm as anxious as you are, William, to see this business put right. But I cannot see why you should make a nuisance of yourself to me. If the little tart had a boy friend at the Flamingo why have the police not found him? And why should he be the same boy as a supposed acquaintance of mine whose name I don't remember? You'll do more harm than good with your conceited, amateur meddling, you know."

I said, "She wasn't a little tart." I was surprised how angry I felt.

Piers grinned. He said, "Have it your own way. But I can't help you. It's not my business. I won't be mixed up with it."

They were almost the same words as those Kate had used to me the other night. I turned on Piers with a remembered anger.

I said, "For God's sake, Piers, how can you stand by? Humphrey is your brother. Have you no feeling for him? He thinks you have. However vulgar you are and however vain, that must carry some weight with you."

Piers advanced towards me slowly, the burning cigarette in his hand. There was a nasty little silence and his mouth was angry and sullen.

He said, "William, I shouldn't get yourself in too deep if I were you. It might be dangerous. Don't let your conceit, drive you too far. My feelings for Humphrey are my concern, not yours. And I shouldn't waste much pity on him if I were you. Now, get out."

He spat the last three words at me with a deliberate venom which was almost frightening because his voice was pitched so low. I took a step backwards away from him. Piers saw me move and laughed gently. He said, in his old manner, "Now run along, dear boy. Can't you see the old gentleman needs his sleep?"

I went, troubled by a sense of failure, wondering whether it might not have been stupidity on my part to think that Piers might have known the boy. It was important that I should not let my own feelings about Piers cloud my judgment; I had no evidence to prove that he had anything to do with it at all.

I drove the car slowly away from the flat, down to Marble Arch. Then I went to The Odd Flamingo.

I wondered, afterwards, why I had not gone there in the first place. It would have been the logical thing to do.

It was hotter than ever in the underground room; the band was absent and there were few customers. The man behind the bar did not seem to recognise me; he gave me the beer I asked for and went on polishing his glasses.

Carl was sitting at a table by himself. His little face was wizened and brown above a pale pink shirt. He had a Pekinese on his lap and he was feeding it with biscuits. It was a pretty little creature with silken saffron-coloured hair.

When I spoke to him he started with what seemed to be genuine alarm. His little eyes were shifty and I thought that he would have preferred not to recognise me. Then he gave me a stiff kind of grin and said with hideous archness, "*Do* go away. Rowley will be here in a minute and he is in *such* a nasty, jealous mood."

The archness was a failure; he was too obviously scared. I said, "Never mind about Rowley. I want you to tell me where I can find Jimmie."

He did not look at me. "Jimmie?" he said. He wasn't a very good actor.

I said, "The boy who knew Rose."

He looked unhappily round the room and then up at me. He said, "I don't know you. Why are you bothering me? I don't know who you are talking about."

He spoke deliberately loudly. The barman put down the glass he was polishing and stood behind the counter looking at us like a sullen watchdog.

Then Carl got up from the table. He was little and lithe and he moved very quickly. He was up the stairs and a hundred yards down the street before I caught him up. We stood in the doorway of a shop and he pressed himself against the plate glass as if he thought it would give him protection. The little dog whined in the shelter of his arm.

He said pleadingly, "Please go away. I don't want to talk to you. Rowley says I must keep out of it. I'm a fool, you see. No one tells me anything. I haven't anything to tell you. *Please.*"

I said, "I'll go away when you tell me what I want to know. Where I can find Jimmie."

He was almost crying. He said, "Rowley says I must be careful.

Look what happened to Jasmine? Such a sweet creature. If I tell you, will you really go away?"

I said, "I promise I will."

His bright eyes were hunted. I found him both distasteful and pathetic. He said, "His name is Callaghan. He lives in the Sandown Road. I don't know the number but it's near the end, on the right. Will you let me go now?"

I said, "Yes. But why must you be careful?"

He repeated, like a child, "Rowley says so. Rowley says I'm a fool. Kate knows. Kate knows why."

Fear had done something to his face; it no longer seemed human. He ducked under my arm and scurried up the road like a little, frightened animal. The dog's bottom bounced absurdly under his arm; with his free hand he held up his trousers which were too long for him and tripped him up.

Kate was in. She said she was pleased to see me but she didn't seem too convinced about it. She looked plain and tired and there was a nervous twitch to her mouth. Her voice was unnatural and sharp; talking to her was like talking to a stranger.

I think that if I had been, in a more normal frame of mind she would have told me nothing. But I was frightened and in a hurry. I remember that? I talked excitedly and probably incoherently. I told her that I had seen Carl and that he had been afraid to talk to me. I told her about Rose. I said that the police thought her dead and that I did not believe them. That I wanted to find her. That I had to find her.

She said, sadly, I think, "Are you in love with her, Willy?"

It was a simple enough question; I was surprised that it should embarrass me so much.

I said, "How can I be in love with her? I've only seen her once."

She said, "Not in love with her in an ordinary sense. But in love with the idea of her. You think her innocent, don't you? Can she be as innocent as all that?"

I said, "I believe so. Silly, perhaps. Young and foolhardy. But innocent."

She looked at me for a little with unhappy eyes. Then she said, "If it is really important to you, Willy, then I'll tell you about Piers. And about Carl."

She looked down at her lap and pleated the stuff of her skirt between her fingers and told me what she knew.

It was, as I had half-expected, a very dreary piece of nastiness.

She had met Piers about a year after she had first come to London and had gone to the Slade with the help of a scholarship. Her parents had died within a few months of each other and she was unhappy and alone although her family life, when they had been alive, had been peculiarly loveless. Her mother had been a petulant semi-invalid and her father had been at home so rarely that he had been a distant figure regarded with more wariness than affection.

In spite of this their deaths had left her rootless and without friends. It must have been a bad time for her although she did not say so; indeed, she went out of her way to make the lonely child that she must have been appear both worthless and silly. It was almost as though she were too proud to ask for any kind of special pleading.

When she had met Piers he had been kind to her. He had treated her with a kind of amused contempt that had endorsed her own bad opinion of herself and that, in a curious way, comforted her. She knew that the kind of life he led was, by all accepted standards, wrong, but none of those standards seemed quite real to her. She had no memory of happiness or security that might have given them meaning.

Piers had taken her into a casual, shallow-rooted society in which everyone was pleasant to her. The people she met were generous and tolerant with their time and their money, they were easily contemptuous of dullness and convention. After a time she became Piers's mistress, not because she loved him, but because it seemed to be expected of her.

Most of this I already knew but until this moment she had never talked to me so frankly about it. Perhaps I had never given her a chance. She had always been shy of talking about herself; I had learned about her affair with Piers from Piers himself sometime

119

after I had known that I loved her and wanted to marry her. It had been too great a blow to my love and my pride for me to feel any desire for understanding.

Then she told me something that I had not known. Piers peddled drugs. He got the stuff from some source she knew nothing about and disposed of it to a small circle of acquaintances. He did not take drugs himself and she thought that he did not do it entirely for profit.

She said, "It always seemed to make it worse, somehow. That he made so little money out of it, I mean. He did it because it gave him a feeling of power, I think."

She had taken the stuff herself. She did not say when she had begun to do so but I assumed that it was some time after I had known her. Piers had told her that there was no danger. She had not believed him but she had taken the stuff just the same. Afterwards, when she could not do without it, he had made it hard for her.

She said, "He would say that I couldn't have any more. He said it was for my own good, but it wasn't that. He wanted me to have to beg for it, to go down on my knees to him. He knew that while I was like that I couldn't do without him and that was what he wanted. Not because he loved me or valued me in any way but just because he liked to feel that I was tied to him. He wants, always, to be the centre of things. He's not much liked and he needs to be liked. It's necessary to his vanity. He used to make me run errands for him before he would let me have the stuff. I used to take it to the Flamingo in my handbag and deliver it to the people there."

I said, astonished that my voice should sound so steady, "But you gave it up, didn't you"

"Twice. The first time I went into a nursing home and it didn't work. When I came out I still couldn't do without it. I went back to Piers. He wouldn't have anything to do with me. I threatened to give him up to the police if he wouldn't help me and he laughed and said that I was as much involved as he was. That I'd delivered the stuff to people who had no idea that he was mixed up in it at all. Then he said that if I didn't get out of the flat he'd call the police himself. He would have done—he's so vain that he wouldn't think there was any danger for him. I wasn't exactly dignified. I screamed at him and at one point I went for him with a knife. I think I wanted to kill him. And he only laughed at me. In the end I realised that he meant what he said—that he'd finished with me. I was no fun for him any more. He'd enjoyed watching me destroy myself and now the process was complete he no longer found me amusing. He pushed me out of the flat and locked the door. I shouted and banged on the door until I was too tired to care any more, but he didn't answer me. Then I went away and Carl took me back to the nursing home. They tried to make me say where I got the drugs but I wouldn't. They cured me and they let me out about three months ago. They were very good. They even found me a job. My boss knows all about me; I think he rather enjoys having an ex-addict about the place. It makes him feel all noble and Christian. It's nice for him."

She sounded very bitter and she had gone alarmingly pale.

I tried not to look at her. I said, "Who did you give the drugs to?"

"Most of the people at the Flamingo. Nowhere else. The staff and the people who go there. Carl, of course. That's why he's so scared, I imagine. He knows Callaghan was a sort of protege of Piers, and I suppose he thinks that if he says anything he shouldn't that Piers will cut off his supplies. Piers has a controlling interest in the Flamingo, you know."

I said, "Did Jimmie Callaghan take the stuff?"

"I think so. He didn't start going to the club until after I'd gone into hospital for the second time. At least, he may have done, but I didn't notice him until I came out. He was in the Flamingo with Piers the first time I saw him. He's a nice-looking boy. Piers likes young boys, and not for the usual reason. Just because they're easier to corrupt."

Her voice was hard and dry with anger.

I said, "Why in Heaven's name did you go on going there?"

She said, with a kind of bravado that bordered on tears, "I was too deeply in, Willy. I told myself that I went there just to make sure that I was safe, that it was all over. But it wasn't the reason. By then it was the only sort of place and the only sort of people that I wanted to know. I'm not happy with ordinary, decent people any more. They make me dislike myself too much."

I didn't want her to get introspective. I said, "And Rose and Jasmine? Were they mixed up in this business?"

She shook her head. "I don't think so. Piers wouldn't have thought them safe enough. Though they were mixed up with Jimmie's gang right enough."

I said, "Gang?"

"It's just a way of speaking. They were a lot of young thugs who went about together. They were good ground for someone like Piers. They listened to his patter, you see, and thought he was God."

I asked her about Humphrey and she shook her head.

"Not Humphrey. I'm sure about that. I don't think Piers would want to do him that kind of harm."

I said, "He's done him harm enough. He made him lie to the police."

She looked uncertain. "I don't understand that. I never did. You see, I know that Piers wasn't at home when he said he was. I know, because I went to his flat some time after midnight on the night the girl was killed."

She looked at me miserably. "It was for Carl. Not for me. Do you remember how drunk he was at the club? He'd run out of the stuff and he wanted it badly. He'd been to see Piers but he wasn't in so he'd come to the Flamingo to look for him there. When he couldn't find Piers he got drunk but it didn't help. It never does. After you left the club he was so ill that I took him home. I tried to make him quiet but it wasn't any good so that in the end I said that I would get the stuff for him. He's a nice little man and he'd been kind to me. I went to Piers's flat. I remember the time because the clock struck midnight when I went into the house and he wasn't there. I waited for about twenty minutes and he didn't come. I remember that I thought it was funny because he usually goes home so early."

I said, "Perhaps he wanted the police to think he *was* at home. Perhaps he wanted the alibi for himself and not for Humphrey."

She stared at me. "But why? He wouldn't have wanted Humphrey to get into trouble. He *loves* him, Willy. As much as he loves anyone."

"Did he know about Rose?"

She nodded. "Yes, he knew. I know that because the first time I saw her I was with Piers. She came into the club with Jimmie and the rest of the boys and Piers told me who she was. I remember because he laughed and said, 'That's my brother's little whore.'"

I said, "You nearly told me that once before. Look—if Piers knew about Rose, then he must have known that it would look bad for Humphrey if she disappeared. Why should he have made it worse for him with a lie?"

She looked distressed. "It may not have seemed so awful for him. To lie to the police, I mean. And anyway ..." She stopped and looked confused.

"Go on," I said.

"I was going to say that it wasn't Rose who was murdered. It was Jasmine. And maybe Piers had no reason to think that Humphrey had had anything to do with *her*. So you see it might not have mattered if the police found out that Humphrey had lied about the time he came home. Only of course that doesn't make sense because no one knew that it wasn't Rose who was dead, until afterwards."

I said, with a cold feeling of horror, "But suppose Piers *did* know that it was Jasmine and not Rose who was dead? Then it would have been a reasonable risk, wouldn't it? If the police accepted the fact that Humphrey was back at the flat just after twelve because Piers had said he was, then they would assume that Piers was there also. So he would be safe. And if they *did* find out—well then, Humphrey was only, being rather stupid and silly in lying to them. No more. Because it wasn't Rose who was dead but a girl that he did not know and had no reason to kill. It would have worked, you see, if they hadn't found Rose's handbag by the canal. That was what put them on to Humphrey in the first place."

She said, "Do you think that Piers killed her, then?"

My hands were sweating and I wiped them with my handkerchief. I said, "Oh, God, how should I know? If I say he might have killed her it will only be wishful thinking because I hate him so. Why should he kill her?"

She screwed up her mouth and said, in a tentative, unhappy way, "I don't think you would need to go far to find a reason. Not among people like that."

The acceptance and the despair in her voice touched me like a cold finger. It brought into sharp relief for me the horror and the shabbiness of a world she knew too well. She looked at me with a kind of shame in her eyes as if she were suddenly aware of the depth of her own private knowledge.

She said, with difficulty, "Willy, are you going to the police? Have you enough to go on, I mean?"

I knew that if I said that I must go to the police she would tell them all she knew and not count the cost to herself.

I said, "I don't want you to be mixed up in it. There may be no need. It wouldn't be pleasant, you know."

She said, with sharp anger, "Don't be a bloody fool." And then, more gently, "You don't have to be quixotic about me, Willy."

She turned away from me and I was conscious, although I could not see her face, of the extent of her humiliation and self-disgust. Her air of careful assurance had gone and without it she was painfully vulnerable. Her voice cracked with the effort of sounding ordinary and casual and shot several tones higher.

She said, "Willy, you don't have to mind about things being pleasant for me. I haven't much to lose."

I suppose that I could have gone up to her and taken her in my arms. It might have helped her a little just then because she was lonely and in need of love. But I couldn't do it. I didn't want to touch her. Instead, I delivered a little homily about starting a new life. It was sincere and well-meant but it sounded as flat as a cold omelette. The only good it did was to give her time to collect the shreds of her dignity. By the time I had finished her eyes were mocking me.

She said, "Dear Willy, I'm sorry that I went emotional on you. It's really your own fault; you brought back my blameless girlhood. But I'm not repentant, you see. I'm a bad bitch, and not ashamed."

Her voice was bright and hard. I think I apologised unsteadily, and we stared at each other for a moment or two.

Then I asked her, to gloss over a bad moment, whether there was anyone else at the club that the girls had known. She said that she didn't know who their friends were. That she had been out of touch.

I remembered what Mrs. Castle had said about an old man who had died.

She said, "You mean old Menhennet. He was quite a character. He'd been going to the Flamingo for years. He was a filthy old man. He smelt and his trousers were tied up with string. He was a bit pathetic in his way. He was a kind of Ancient Mariner—he used to button-hole people and tell them what a wag he'd been in his younger days. He didn't drink much—he used to sit at a table near the band and mumble away to himself. I think the girls knew him. They were talking to him one evening, I remember. I thought they were doing it for a lark. I remember that we laughed about it because he couldn't take his eyes off them. Afterwards I was sorry that I'd laughed."

I asked her why and she went pink. She said, "Partly because it was unkind. He could help being dirty but he couldn't help being old and a bore. And because he did one rather sweet thing. He came into the club one evening when there were a lot of people there and he went up to your Rose. She was sitting with Jimmie and his friends and they were all pretty drunk. He pulled a bunch of violets out of his pocket and gave them to Rose. They were very dead violets—they looked as if they'd been in his pocket for days. Of course they all thought it was terribly funny. Except Rose. She smiled at him, she was a kind-looking child. But the others laughed and he went out of the club mumbling to himself. I don't think he came in again. He died—they were talking about it at the bar when I went in a few weeks ago. They stopped talking as soon as they saw me, I'm not in with them any more, you see. So I don't know any more—except that he is dead."

I said, "I don't suppose there is any more to it than that."

She said, "No, I don't suppose there is," and we both looked at the floor. I said good-bye to her and thanked her in a stilted way. I think that she was glad to see me go.

When I had left her I stood on the Embankment. There was no breeze and along the gutters the dirty paper lay still in the hot dust.

I was weary and appallingly ashamed. My hands were hot and dirty and I rubbed at them with my handkerchief in a kind of frantic anxiety as if it were immensely important that they should be clean. Then I realised that it was a pointless thing to do so I put the grubby handkerchief away and got into the car and drove away.

Chapter Ten

The sandown road was long and grey and ugly; even on this hot day it seemed to provide a channel for a chill, unpleasant wind. At the end farthest from the canal the houses were well-kept and clean; half way along they declined dramatically both in cleanliness and respectability. By the time I reached the canal the street seemed both dirty and disreputable; I parked my car round the corner by the canal feeling that it would be less noticeable there. When I had locked the car, I stood for a moment by the fence that walled off the canal. It was quite low and I could look over it.

The water was brown and thick with leaves and sludge; it gave off a sweet, rotten smell. About two hundred yards away was the bridge where Jasmine's body had been found; it was an ugly, Victorian affair, high and rectangular, like the footbridges that span railway lines. There were some boys playing on the bank; I could hear their voices, shrill and sharp and cockney in the stillness of the late afternoon. I remembered that it had been boys who had found the girl's drowned body.

I felt a sudden upsurge of pity and of horror. I thought, with a pain that was almost physical, of the life cut short, the terror and the surprise. I wondered if she had known she was going to die or if the blow on the head had come too suddenly for fear. I remembered the photograph of Jasmine that her mother had shown me, and I wondered what she had looked like when they had taken her from the river.

I was very cold in spite of the thundery heat. I left the canal and walked into the road. Then I saw Piers. He came down the steps of a house just ahead of me. He was hatless and he seemed to be in a hurry. He strutted up the street, away from me, like an angry barnyard cock.

I climbed the steps of the house he had just left and examined the greasy line of cards beneath the bell-push by the open door.

The bottom card read, "Callaghan. Flat Four."

I went in. The hall was crowded with bicycles and battered perambulators. A suitcase stood at the bottom of the bare, wooden stairs and I almost fell over it. I climbed the stairs slowly.

The door was on the second landing. As I reached it, it jerked open violently and a man stood on the threshold. He was a very young man. His hair was like white silk and his eyes were wide and blue and sullen. He wore a loose linen jacket and a flowing tartan tie. Except for the clothes he looked like a clean public schoolboy. He held a suitcase in one hand and with the other he pressed a handkerchief to his mouth.

He said, "What d'you want?" His voice was uneducated but surprisingly soft and musical.

I said, "I want to speak to Mr. Callaghan."

Neither then, nor later, did I understand why he acted as he did. There was a spurt of pure panic in his eyes; he dropped the handkerchief and the blood from his cut mouth ran down his chin and on to his collar. His arm moved forwards and upwards and the heavy suitcase caught me on the side of the head so that I reeled backwards against the banister rail and fell. I put my arm up to defend my face but there was no second blow. The boy ran lightly down the stairs and his feet clattered on the stone of the steps outside.

I lay where I had fallen for about a minute. I got slowly to my feet and felt a sharp pain in my head, just above the eye. I held tightly to the banister rail and went down the stairs. When I reached the street it was hot and empty except for two women gossiping on the opposite pavement. I went back into the house and climbed the stairs and went into the room the boy had left.

It was a large, high room, furnished shabbily with a bed, a wardrobe and a few chairs. There was a gas ring with a mess of dried fat about its base and a washbasin with a rough, wooden cover. The room was quite bare of personal possessions.

Someone came into the room behind me. I turned and saw a vast woman with a body that bulged and billowed beneath a dirty, flowered apron. She had unpleasant eyes and a mouth with almost no lips at all.

She said, "What was you wanting?"

I said, "I was looking for Jimmie Callaghan," and I put my hand up to my head. It came away tacky and dark with blood.

The woman said, "You've cut yer 'ead. Did 'e do that?"

I said dully, "There must have been an iron corner to the thing," and felt for my handkerchief.

She said, "Best come downstairs and I'll give you a lend of a bandage."

I followed her and she took me down to the basement and produced a bandage and some warm water. She peered eagerly at the cut.

"That's nasty," she said. "Looks as if you'll want a stitch."

She spoke with some satisfaction. Then she said, "You won't find Jimmie 'ere. Give 'im notice, I did, weeks ago. Only just got 'im out. Waiting for the rent, see. Couldn't let 'im go without the rent, now could I?"

I shook my head stupidly. She said, "You look as if you could do with a cuppa." She put a kettle on the stove and went on. "Not that I was sorry to, see the back of 'im, I can tell you. Didn't fancy the company 'e was keeping, though 'e didn't reelly give me cause to complain—not until a few weeks back. Then I saw me chance and I took it."

I said, "What sort of a man is he?"

"Not a man, reelly. More of a boy. He wasn't no worse than most boys when 'e come 'ere. I've got boys meself and I know what they're like. Then 'e got into bad company, started throwing 'is money about, see, and we 'ad the police 'ere. Lets a house down, that sort of thing. Not that I said anything about that. After all, 'e paid his rent regular, which is more than I could say for some of the others."

"You think he was up to something wrong?" I said.

The pain in my head was very sharp.

She shrugged her huge shoulders. She seemed as boneless as a jelly fish. The kettle came to the boil and she made the tea.

"Reelly, I don't know." She turned on me with curiosity. "What d'you want to know for?"

I told her a little of the truth. I said I was looking for a girl. I said that I thought she had known Jimmie Callaghan. I hinted, gently, that she might also have known Jasmine Castle, the girl they had found dead in the canal.

Her eyes shone with a peculiarly repulsive excitement. She knew all about Jasmine Castle. The neighbourhood had talked of nothing else. She added a few details that I had not heard and had no wish to hear.

"But it wasn't Jimmie's girl," she said. "I saw her photo in the papers, so I know."

"What was Jimmie's girl like?" I asked. "What was her name?"

She shook her head. She didn't know the name, but she had seen the girl.

"She was a little thing," she said. "Ever so pretty, though she 'adn't much colour to 'er, if you know what I mean. Nicely spoken she was, quite the lady. She gave me a box of chocolates once. She was too good for that Jimmie. Big black eyes she had like grapes. It was because of her that I gave 'im notice."

After a little prompting she told me the story. She had no liking for Jimmie.

She was vague about the date but it seemed as if it had all happened about a fortnight before Rose had come to London on that fatal final visit. The landlady had been to the pictures and she had come home when the cinema closed, at about eleven o'clock. She would ordinarily have gone straight down to her basement but there had been a leak in the cistern of the first floor lavatory and the plumber had promised to come in that evening and put it right. So she panted up the stairs to see if he had done so. After she had come out of the lavatory she had heard Jimmie shouting at his girl on the floor above. She had been annoyed because of the other tenants but she would have done nothing about it beyond speaking to Jimmie in the morning if she had not heard the girl scream.

It was a high-pitched scream, broken off in the middle with frightening suddenness. The woman had heaved herself up the next flight of stairs and gone into the room and closed the door behind her.

They were standing by the window. Jimmie had his hands round the girl's throat and he was shaking her backwards and forwards. He was saying, over and over again in a kind of angry mutter, "You won't get out of it this way. I'll see you in hell first."

It was an unexpected and terrifying scene; it was to the woman's credit that she acted as she did. She did not call for help; she went to the window and dragged the boy away. It was not easy; his fingers were crooked round the girl's throat as though he could not let her go.

When they were separated at last he stared at his landlady as though he did not really see her. His eyes were bloodshot and half-closed. He was very pale and almost quite drunk. He was swaying a little as though he could not stand upright.

The girl had fallen back against the window sill. She was cringing a little and there were dark marks on her neck but she seemed, after a moment, to be completely calm and self-possessed. She said with an odd, bright smile, as if nothing out of the way had happened:

"I really am so sorry to trouble you. It wasn't anything. Jimmie got upset at something I told him. He didn't mean to hurt me."

Rose—I was quite sure it was Rose—was trying hard to put a good face on it, to make it seem like an ordinary lovers' quarrel. It was gallant and useless and pathetic. She thought, I suppose, that it wasn't quite nice to be found with a young man who was trying to kill her; I thought of her defending her sad little notions of respectability and it wrung my heart.

Jimmie said, "If you squeal, you bitch, I'll get you if I swing for it."

The woman pushed in front of them with a vague idea of protecting Rose. She spoke of the girl all the time with what seemed, in her, unusual gentleness. She had said to Rose, "I think you'd best go, lovey. And if you ask me I shouldn't come back."

Rose said, "Where can I go?"

It was a cry of despair. She had gone very white. And then her control went. She started to shake all over and she clutched with both hands at the window sill as if to prevent herself from falling.

She said, "You mustn't blame him too much. You mustn't tell anyone. It's all my fault. I gave him a shock." A bright blush spread over her face and throat. "It was something I had to tell him."

The landlady said, "Whatever you done there's no call for him to go murdering you. If you ask me, it's a case for the police."

She said piteously, "Oh, no. Not the police. You see it really *was* awful what I had to tell him. I'm going to have a baby. Someone else's baby."

The boy made a move towards her. He said, "She's a lying little sow." His voice was both bitter and thoroughly surprised as though he had not properly understood before. He put his hands to his head and sat down.

The girl looked at him, her eyes enormous in her small face and with a fixed, frightened smile.

She said, "It's true, isn't it, Jimmie? You haven't forgotten what I told you, have you?"

There was a kind of unhappy bewilderment on the boy's face. He said, "I'll get you for this. See if I don't."

There was no real menace in his voice. He got up from his chair looking as if he were going to cry. He moved uncertainly towards Rose, spat a filthy word at her and left the room.

The woman took Rose down to her basement room. She gave her a cup of tea and witch hazel for her throat. When Rose had drunk the tea she had cried a little.

The woman said, "I felt reel sorry for her, I can tell you. Such a pretty, soft little thing she was. And it was such a sad story, just like the pictures. You see, there was this other man—he was a lot older than she was and ever so handsome and he was in love with her. They couldn't get married because he was married already. But she was going to have his baby, see? And when she told him about it 'e wouldn't 'ave any more to do with her. She didn't know what to do—she was scared to tell her mother. Then she'd met this Jimmie and 'e was ever so much in love with 'er too. Only she couldn't forget the other man, see? And she couldn't marry Jimmie, not without telling him about the baby. Poor, silly young thing."

Her hard little eyes had surprising and quite genuine tears in them.

I said, "Have you any idea where Jimmie Callaghan has gone?"

"Back to 'is mum, I reckon. She lives out Staines way."

"Can you find the address?" I asked.

"I 'spect I can. I've got it somewheres. 'E gave it to me once when he went to stay with 'is mum for a couple of weeks. I'll say that for 'im—he's fond of his mum. Thinks the world of 'er."

She rummaged in a blue and white willow pattern mug that stood on a shelf above the stove, and produced a torn envelope with an address written on it in a round, uneducated hand. I asked her if I could take it and put it in my wallet.

As I went out, she said, "I should 'ave a stitch put in that cut, if I were you."

I went to a chemist's shop in the Kilburn High Road. The man washed my head with spirit and said that it would be all right. He pushed the edges of the cut together with a strip of plaster and the place seemed to take on a new lease of pain and throbbed and smarted intolerably. The whole side of my face was stiff and sore.

I sat in the car and wondered whether I ought to go to the police. I didn't want to. They thought her dead; I felt a smouldering resentment against them because they thought her dead.

It was seven o'clock. I looked at the map and decided that it would take me about an hour to get to the address near Staines. I turned the car and drove back towards the canal, over a bridge and into Queensway and the Bays-water Road. I drove fast and I tried not to think.

There was very little traffic on the road once I had got out of Hammersmith and I made better time than I had expected. I stopped at a pub on the way and had a drink and a sandwich.

The house was off the road; it stood alone at the side of some gravel pits that had been abandoned and filled with water. There were scrubby little islands standing up in the water so that the place looked rather like a desolate, natural lake. There was a rubbish shoot just off the road, strewn with tin cans and ancient tyres and heaps of what looked like coffee grounds; it gave off a pungent, sickly smell.

The house was a rickety impermanent affair consisting of a large Nissen hut with a few wooden outbuildings that had been joined on to it haphazardly. It was surrounded by a dirt yard where a few sick-looking chickens scratched at the ground.

The door of the hut was open and I could hear a wireless playing and a child screaming. I went up to the doorway and looked in. The interior was dark after the bright sun. There were two children playing on the threshold; they stopped their game and stared at me, their fingers in their mouths.

One of them shouted, "Mum," and after a minute or so a woman appeared from the back of the hut with a baby clinging on her hip.

She was a tall woman with a big, slack body. She had a round, unlined face and she gave me a curiously sweet, supine smile. I thought that she must have been a pretty girl.

I said, "Are you Mrs. Callaghan?" and she nodded and smiled and said in a gentle Irish voice, "That's my name. If it's my Bridget you've come about, she's got the worms. The doctor said she wasn't to go to school with the worms."

I said, "I haven't come from the school, Mrs. Callaghan. I want to see your son, Jimmie. Is he here?"

Instantly the smile vanished, her whole face tightened up and she said, "What d'you want Jimmie for?"

I said, "I just wanted to ask him some questions. That's all."

She came outside the hut, sweeping the children behind her and closed the door on them. Then she said, "He's not here. What was it you wanted to know?"

She was a bad liar. I said nothing and she went on nervously, "He's a good boy, my Jimmie. There's not many boys who are good to their mums. He's a real good 'un."

She was looking uneasily round her, particularly in the direction of the river which lay some way off across the flat fields, shining like a white, satin ribbon.

I said gently, "I'm not from the police, Mrs. Callaghan."

She said wildly, "Why should I think you was the police? My boy's done nothing. He's a good boy."

She came closer to me. She smelt sour with sweat. The baby she held on her hip was very thin and small; his pale, white head was too big for his midget limbs and there were red sores round his mouth and under his nose.

She said, "If you're that probation officer he was talking about, he's going straight now. Got a good job and doing nicely. He bought me the television last month."

I said, "I'm not a probation officer. I just wanted to see your son. Are you sure you haven't seen him to-day?"

She shook her head; the baby on her hip let out a dreary wail and she bounced it up and down automatically and it went on wailing.

I walked back down the lane to the road and drove the car about a quarter of a mile back towards the town. I went to the lane again and scrambled through the hedge that divided it from the gravel pits. I waited for perhaps half-an-hour.

When the little boy came out of the Nissen hut he wriggled through the hedge some way away from me and ran towards the water. There was an old and leaky punt tied up at the bank. He jumped into it and began to untie the frayed rope. He was so intent on his task that he did not notice me until I spoke to him. Then he looked up, startled but not, apparently, afraid.

He grinned in a friendly way and said, "'Ullo, mister."

He was a very thin little boy, his legs were crooked and shaky as pea-sticks but his eyes were sharp and blue.

I said, "Like to earn half-a-crown?"

He said warily, "What for, mister?" and he glanced towards the hut. We could not be seen from the yard, only the tin roof of the Nissen was visible.

I squatted on my haunches so that my face was on the boy's level. I said, "I want to talk to your brother Jimmie. Is he here?"

The child said, "Are you a flattie?"

"No," I said. "I just want to ask him something."

"Give us the dough, brother," the boy said in a very creditable imitation of an American accent.

I took half-a-crown out of my pocket and held it out to him. He made no move to take it so I flipped the coin into the flat bottom of the boat and he picked it up and put it in his pocket. He sniffed and rubbed his sleeve across his nose.

He said, "'E was 'ere just afore you come. You ain't going to put 'im in the nick, are you?"

"The nick? No, I shouldn't think so."

The boy pointed. "Down the river. In the *Dinky Sue*." Then he giggled. "Cor, I shan't 'alf cop it if mum finds out." He didn't appear to be especially alarmed.

He went back to untying the rope. When he had finished he took a stick out of the bottom of the punt and began to pole himself out into the middle of the water.

Before he went I asked him, "Where is your father? Is he at home?"

At once the child looked both furtive and scared. "No, 'e ain't," he said. He pushed the boat away from the shore. It was something of a triumph for him to move the big punt at all, he was so very small, but he got it across to one of the islands where there was a dump of empty tins and as I went back to the road he was scrambling over the dump, dragging a dark sack behind him.

Chapter Eleven

As I walked to the river the day was dying in a splash of scarlet; the tall poplars were dark and still at the water's edge. Along one side of the river there was a sandy tow-path, on the other the fields ended in an expanse of blue-green rushes. From where I stood, on the bridge, I could see a few small boats tied up at their mooring places on the tow-path side. Except for a long converted landing craft they were all dinghies or small punts.

It was not a pretty part of the river; the fields were flat and there were no houses, probably because the land lay low and flooded in the winter. There was nobody about. I went down off the bridge and on to the tow-path and walked in the direction of the landing craft. It was big and clumsy and painted a dirty grey. The owners had built a permanent gangway from the path; the sound of the wireless came out through the open window and the lights were on. There were people inside, a man and a woman and a couple of children. They were moving about the boat and talking and laughing. Except for the small boats there was nothing else in sight.

I went back to the bridge and crossed the road to the other side. Here there were no boats that could be seen from the bridge but about a hundred yards away the river bent sharply away from the road and the banks were invisible. Looking across the fields I could see the little islands in the gravel pit and the top of the Callaghans' Nissen hut. There was a track through the field and I walked along it, by the side of the river, until it met a clump of bushes and turned inland.

Then I saw the boat. She lay on the opposite bank, snugly hidden among the rushes. She was a small grey craft with a humped cabin, not more than fifteen feet from stem to stern. She looked a very home-made affair. The light was going fast but I could just make out the name on the bows. It was the *Dinky Sue*.

There was no immediately obvious way of getting to her. I looked for a dinghy and then I saw that it was tied up to the boat, rising and falling on the water. I could hear the faint creak of the rope.

I went back to the bridge and crossed to the other side, pushing my way through a thin thorn, hedge that fenced the field from the road. Even now, in summer, next to the river the ground was soggy underfoot. I was surprised to find how near I was to the gravel pit; I could see the scrubby islands although the Nissen hut was hidden behind the trees.

I walked along the river, the reeds between me and the water, until I hit the path. I could not see the boat because the high rushes screened the river. The path led into the reeds; it was the merest thread of a path.

I looked behind me and saw a caravan site further away from the road between the pits and the river. I could not see very well but I thought there were four or five caravans, pitched close together. There was a light shining in one of them; I could see a man moving about outside and I heard, faintly, a child crying.

It took away a little from the crushing sense of loneliness that had descended upon me.

I went along the path through the reeds and came upon the boat and the water's edge. The craft was moored to a gravel beach that was little more than a shallow bite out of the river bank.

Close to, the boat was squat and clumsy and not very sound. It listed sideways a little as though it was aground on the gravel. There were tiny windows in the side of the cabin; they were tightly covered by flowered curtains.

I waded up to my knees in water that was surprisingly cold. I stepped over the gunwale and shook the handle of the cabin door. It was locked.

I shouted, "Hullo, there," and my voice sounded hollow and strange in the silence of the evening.

If Callaghan had been there he was not there now. I waited for a moment and then I let myself down into the water and stepped back on to the little beach. I stooped down to wring the water out of my trousers wishing, regretfully, that I had not been wearing my best light suit.

As I straightened up I saw Jimmie Callaghan standing above me on the bank.

He said, "That's my boat. What d'you want?"

He looked out of place by the silent river, a little London spiv in bright yellow shoes. The soft dusk made his face look ridiculously young and, in a curious way, almost vulnerable.

He said, "What have you come here for?"

I said, "I might also ask what you hit me for. I haven't come about that. I wanted to ask you some questions."

The boy peered at me. In the quiet and the uncertain light it all seemed oddly unreal.

I said, "I believe you know Rose Blacker. I want to find her."

The boy stepped backwards; in his voice there was a high note of alarm. He said, "I dunno who you're talking about. Are you a copper?"

I said, "No, I'm not a policeman. You've no reason to be afraid of me."

He said, contemptuously, "'Course I'm not afraid. What d'you take me for?" He swaggered a little, throwing up his chin, his hands in his pockets.

I said, "You know where she is, don't you?"

He said, "If I did, I wouldn't tell you, see? Why should I? Anyway I ain't seen her in weeks. Now get away from my boat or I'll let you have it where it hurts."

I said, "I think you can tell me something, can't you? I'll make it worth your while."

The boy laughed. "Not 'alf you won't. I can't tell you anything, see? Now get away from my boat."

I hesitated a moment. Then I said, "What did Mr. Stone have to say to you this afternoon before you left London?"

Callaghan said nothing and then he spat out a foul word with extraordinarily concentrated vindictiveness. After that he said, "We had a row. He tried to take the mickey out of me. I don't let people take the mickey out of me, see? He won't do it again in a hurry."

I said, "What did he want?"

"I'm not telling you, see? It ain't none of your bloody business, Mister long nose. You get away from my boat. I'm not telling you again."

I said, as equably as I could, "Why did he hit you?"

The boy made an odd, animal sound, like an angry whimper. He made a swift movement in the half-dark and I saw that he had an automatic in his hand.

He said, "If you don't get away from my boat I'll blow a hole in your guts."

The sensation of unreality grew stronger. I might have been in the middle of a gangster film; the boy's words had just that kind of feel about them. I found, and it surprised me, that I was not in the least afraid.

I said, "It's silly to talk like that. It would be murder, you know."

He spat. He said, with a self-conscious air, "Go on, get out of it, brother. Or I'll let you have it, see? I'm not afraid of the cops."

I said, "What have you got in your boat that you don't want me to see?"

He said, "Get out," in a high, goaded whisper. He raised the hand with the gun in it and I half fell, half threw myself forward and tackled him round the legs. I felt his knees buckle and we toppled together on to the hard little beach. The boy gave a small, sobbing cry as his head hit the stones; it was with enormous relief that I realised the gun had not gone off.

I was heavier than Callaghan and in good condition but I was neither so young, nor so agile. We struggled clumsily for a moment or two and then I got a grip on the boy by both arms, holding him just above the elbows. The bones of his arms felt astonishingly fragile beneath my hands and I felt, exultantly, that I had him where I wanted him. Then he twisted like a snake beneath me and wriggled one leg free of my weight. The blow caught me in the stomach and for a moment the pain left me helpless. There were scarlet blotches in front of my eyes; I rolled clear of the boy, doubled up and gasping, and slipped half into the water. I wondered, in spite of the pain, what had happened to the gun and whether he would really use it. For a brief moment I did not care very much whether he did or not.

The cold water eased the agony a little and I crawled on my hands and knees out of the river. I vomited on to the gravel and felt better. When I looked up the boy had gone. For a moment I felt only relief and then I was afraid that I would lose him. I managed to stand upright and I went along the path a little way until I could see the boy dimly, running across the fields. It was, by now, almost entirely dark, but I could see the loose, light-covered coat. He seemed to be making for the caravans.

In my present state it was useless to go after him. I doubted whether it would be much good anyway; my encounters with him to date had been almost ludicrously unsuccessful. I went back to the beach to look for the gun; I could not think that he would have bolted if he had not dropped it.

I had a fountain-pen torch and I searched the gravel with its needle beam but there was no sign of the gun. I crouched by the water and felt in the river; at the edge the bed sloped gently and it was quite shallow. I found it after about five minutes' blind groping and took it out of the water and dried it on my handkerchief. I took out the magazine and pulled back the bolt. Both the magazine and the chamber were empty.

I stood up and something tinkled by my shoe. It was a small padlock key. I weighed it in my hand for a moment and then I waded into the water and climbed on to the boat. The key fitted the padlock on the cabin door.

Inside the cabin it was hot and dark and there was a strong, sickly smell. The roof was low, I hit my head and swore, peering into the thick blackness.

I lit my torch and shone it round the cramped space. There was an oil lamp hanging from the roof and there was someone lying on the bunk against the wall.

I said, "Hullo, who is it?" and stumbled across the cabin, kicking over a clanking bucket, and shone the torch on to the face on the pillow.

For a moment I did not recognise her and then she opened her enormous eyes and stared at me. The eyes were blank and unseeing, she moved her head fretfully on the pillow as if the light was hurting her.

I said, unbelieving, "Rose," and she gave a long, tired sigh and closed her eyes again.

I lit the lamp after a great deal of trouble; the wick was nearly worn down and had to be coaxed before it would ignite. When it was lit at last it filled the tiny cabin with a clear, soft glow. There was a table by the bunk: with a glass of water on it and an empty cup with tea dregs in it. The whole place was quite clean and the linen on the bunk looked fresh and comfortable.

I went up to the bunk and I was shocked to see how ill she looked. Her face was an odd, greyish colour and her lips were parted and pale with a yellow line round the mouth. She was breathing lightly, so lightly that the bedclothes barely moved. The hand that lay outside the cover was frighteningly thin; I took her wrist and tried to feel her pulse but I wasn't quite sure how to set about it. I called her name and she opened her eyes and looked at me. Without the light shining on her face, she looked more normal.

I said, "Rose." She moved her lips as if she were trying to say something. Then she turned her head on the pillow and looked at the table by the bunk.

I raised her shoulders gently and held the glass to her lips. She drank a little of the water and the rest ran down her chin on to the bedclothes.

I said, "Rose, who brought you here? Who's been looking after you?"

She said, with a pitiable effort, "Jimmie. He's here. There was a woman."

I said, "Have you seen a doctor?"

She shook her head slowly, "I lost my baby," she said.

Her skin, when I touched her, was hot and dry; when I laid her back on the bed she looked completely exhausted and even more grey. She was quite unlike my memory of her; she no longer looked young and she smelt like a sick animal.

I put my head close to the pillow. I said, "Rose, listen to me. We've all been looking for you—your mother and everyone else. I'm going away now but I'll come back and take you where you'll be properly looked after."

She gave no sign that she had heard what I said and she did not move. Then, after a moment of silence she looked at me with desperate appeal and said, "No. No, you mustn't do that. They'll do for me. I want to stay. Go away now. Go away."

The last words were a high, wailing cry; she half-raised herself from the pillow, gasping and clutching at my sleeve with her thin, hot hand. There was extreme terror on her face and in her eyes. I was frightened for her.

I said, "Of course I'll go away. There's nothing to be frightened about. Go to sleep now, there's a good child."

She sighed and fell back on the pillow. I wondered if there was anything I could do for her but it seemed almost as if she had gone to sleep. Her eyes were closed and the breath came through her lips in a staccato fashion. I pulled the bedclothes gently round her, turned the wick of the oil lamp low and left the cabin.

I fastened the padlock and put the key in my pocket. Standing on the creaking deck I knew that I did not want to leave her there alone. I wished that I knew how ill she was and then I wondered if she were going to die.

I swung myself off the boat into the water and ran along the path, forgetting the ache in my head and the pain in my stomach.

The moon was coming up and giving a little light so that I saw Jimmie Callaghan quite clearly as I ran towards the lane that led from the Nissen hut to the road. I had made for the lane because it was the quickest way back to the car; I had not thought that Callaghan might be waiting for me there. He was standing quite motionless in front of the dark hedge, his hands in the pocket of his light jacket.

I slowed my pace uncertainly; the boy did not move or speak until we were perhaps twenty yards apart. What happened then was wholly unexpected; the blow that came from behind and knocked me sprawling on the ground took me completely by surprise. I felt, not afraid, but astonished and bewildered; it was unbelievable that this should happen to me in an English field so near to people and a town. Someone knelt painfully in the small of my back and tied my elbows together and then let me go and rolled me on to my side so that I saw the man who had knocked me down. He was a big man with a flat, angry face. It was the man from the band. The one the barman had called Stan.

Callaghan stood beside the big man and looked down at me. His face was without expression; in the moonlight it looked narrow and mean.

I said, through a mouthful of wet earth, "What the hell do you think you are doing?" I felt absurdly indignant.

Callaghan said, "The same goes for you, mister. Messing about with my boat and my girl."

I thought that he sounded undecided. I said, "Your girl is ill. I think maybe she is dying. She should be in a hospital."

The big man swore at me and kicked me in the side so that the tears came into my eyes.

Callaghan said sharply, "Shut up, Stan." Then he bent down to me, the silver hair hanging lankly in his eyes, and said, "Don't you try any funny business, see? I'm looking after her all right. She's my girl."

He sounded both savage and uncertain. I said, "She can't be all right in that boat. Do you want her to die?"

The boy's face twisted with an emotion that I did not understand. He knelt down and went, quite gently, through my pockets. He took out my wallet and threw it on the ground. He found the gun and put it in his own pocket and then he found the cabin key. He fumbled with the cord that tied my arms and jerked it free. He said, "Get out of here. And leave me alone or you'll get a bullet in your guts. I'm warnin' you, see?"

I felt that the words he spoke were not his own words but somehow second-hand. I was not clear why they were letting me go; later I realised that there was nothing else, short of killing me,

144

that they could have done. And that, even then, they were not prepared to do.

I got to my feet and stumbled away from them, towards the lane. As I squeezed through a gap in the hedge I heard them running. I was afraid then, not for myself, but for Rose.

The car was where I had left it; it took me nearly a minute to get the ignition key into the hole because my hands were shaking so. I drove towards the town and stopped at the first telephone box and called the police. The operator put me on to the local branch; it seemed to me, in my agitation, that they were unbearably slow in understanding what I wanted them to do. In the end they said that they would come and that they would bring an ambulance. The officer at the station was maddeningly calm and unconcerned. I said that I would go back to the boat and wait for them there.

When I reached the bridge I stopped the car and went into the field. It was very quiet and I could hear the thumping of my own heart. The cabin door was open sending a shaft of sickly light across the water. I climbed on to the deck and looked in. Bending over the bunk was a man in a long black robe.

I had a long moment of nightmarish terror and then the priest turned towards me and I saw his mild, sane face and the worried, myopic eyes.

What Callaghan had done seemed almost inexplicably out of character. After the police had come, and the ambulance, and they had carried Rose gently from the boat, the priest told me about it.

Callaghan had stopped him in the road, near to the bridge. The priest had been on his bicycle; he had heard the boy shouting to him and then he had seen him, running along the white road, his jacket flying loose, stumbling as he ran. The priest had recognised him as he came closer he had been in the parish a long time, almost as long as the boy had been alive. He had a good memory.

The boy had been choking and out of breath. It was some minutes before the man had understood what he was trying to say. Callaghan had got it out in the end; he said that there was a girl ill, perhaps dying, in a boat by the river. She was a Catholic and he thought that the priest should come. He had sounded desperate, almost in anguish.

It was anyone's guess, of course, why he should have acted like that. He was a Catholic himself but he had not been one in any real sense since he was a boy at his first school. And yet, there he was in his moment of extreme fear, clutching with superstitious fingers at the once familiar black habit.

The priest had listened to him and asked no questions. He had left his bicycle by the hedge and tramped with Callaghan to the boat. He said that the boy was looking over his shoulder all the time as if he was afraid that someone was following him. The priest had asked him what was the matter and Callaghan had said roughly, "That's none of your business. Your business is with my girl, not with me."

He had spoken with deliberate contempt but he had helped the old man on to the boat and stood aside so that he should enter the cabin first.

Rose was lying quite still, her lips drawn back over her teeth, and for a moment the priest had thought that she was dead. Callaghan knelt by the bunk and put his arms round her and suddenly his voice was breaking and warm with love.

He said softly, "Rosie, Rosie—it's all right now. My love, my cherry flower." She did not move and he looked up at the priest with bleak despair. He said, "She ain't going to die?" He got up from his knees and stood back so that the priest could go near to the bunk.

Then the boy said, "He's gone for the doctor. You won't leave her alone till they come?"

His voice was suddenly submissive and pleading as if the memory of an old authority had come back to him. Then, while the priest was busy with Rose and trying to make her more comfortable, he went quickly and without any noise, so that when the man turned to speak to him he was no longer there. It was the last that anyone saw of him until the end.

When the ambulance had gone I offered to take the priest to

146

the police station in the car. I said, because it was bothering me, "I wouldn't have expected him to mind about the girl so much."

He said, "Why shouldn't he mind about her?"

I said, "I don't know. Do you know anything about him?"

He said, "Not much. Is he in trouble? Are you from the police?"

I shook my head. "I'm not a policeman. I don't know whether he is in trouble or not. He is mixed up in something, I think. I don't know how bad it is."

He said, "It is a bad family. The father is always in and out of prison. The mother is an honest sort of woman—or would be if she'd had a chance. I remember the boy."

He hesitated and went on, "He has been up before a juvenile court once, maybe twice. The probation officer came to see me about him. I saw him and talked to him but I don't think I did much good. That sort of boy is hard to reach. Perhaps I didn't try hard enough."

His voice was flat and weary; he took off his glasses and wiped them on his cassock.

We drove along the road until we came to the place where he had left his bicycle. We strapped it on to the luggage grid. I realised then how old a man he was; his hands were coarsely veined and shaky and his movements slow.

As we got back into the car, I said, "What had he done when the probation officer came to see you?"

"He had stolen fruit off a barrow. There were other boys with him but he was the only one who was caught. I saw his mother and she didn't seem to realise what her son had done. She said all the usual things—that it was just a boy's prank and that he went to too many gangster films. It was impossible to make her understand that what he had done was really wrong. He went to the Labour Exchange after that and got a job in London. Quite a good job, I believe, for that kind of boy. He used to send his mother money, he was a good son. I think that I thought he was going straight and I put him from my mind. I should not have done that."

He had an irritatingly gentle voice; he sounded both helpless and very tired. He said, "Why are you interested in him? Are you sure you don't know what he has done?"

I said, "I can't tell you. I don't know. He may not have done anything. I wasn't looking for him, but for the girl."

I drove in silence for a little while and then I told the old man about Rose. Enough to explain my own interest in her and then a little more because I found that I could not stop talking about her. She had become so real and important that Humphrey was, at that moment, a shadowy figure almost without meaning for me.

I found that I was hoping that they would not keep me long at the police station because I wanted to get to the hospital.

When we got to the station I made a statement but they did not keep me long. They told me that Rose had been taken to one of the big London hospitals and that there was a police officer with her. They did not know how she was but they offered to let me use the telephone. I thanked them and said that I would go to the hospital.

I drove to London along the empty roads thinking about her and praying a little.

When I reached the hospital I went into the casualty ward and asked about her. The nurse had only just come on duty but she offered to fetch the house surgeon. I waited for what seemed an interminable time, sitting on the hard bench and staring at the aseptic walls. They brought a drunk into the casualty ward and took him into an inner room. He was crying for his mother, the tears streaming down his dirty, tramp's face, and he went on crying all the time that I was there.

At last the doctor came; he was a young, clean-shaven boy in a white coat. He had a stethoscope hanging round his neck and he fingered it all the time he was talking as though it gave him confidence.

He said that they had made Rose as comfortable as they could and that she was in a small room off a main ward and that a police officer was with her. He tried not to show that he was curious about it all and I liked him for that. He was cautious about her; he said that she had had a miscarriage and that she had a deep pneumonia. In the ordinary way, of course, there would have been nothing to worry about. People didn't die of pneumonia now because of penicillin but her case was more complicated because of the miscarriage and because she had been too long without proper care.

I said, "Do you think she will die?" knowing that it was the only thing I cared about and he looked slightly shocked as though I had asked an improper question.

He said that of course he couldn't say, that there was no certain answer to the question but that she was young and would have every attention. He seemed bothered and embarrassed.

Then he said, "Has she any relatives? Should we get in touch with them? Of course we usually do that sort of thing ourselves when casualties are brought in but as this is a police case I don't know what will have been done."

I told him that I would find out and do what was necessary. I thanked him for his trouble and gave him the telephone number of my club. I wanted to stay at the hospital but I told myself that it was foolish and I should be a nuisance.

I went back to my club and shut myself into a telephone booth. It was a smart little box with a shiny leather seat along one wall. I rang Scotland Yard; I hadn't really expected that Jennings would be there so that it was a surprise when his voice came along the line. It sounded thin and unexpectedly refined, a civil servant's voice.

I said, "Rose has been found. She's safe." I think that I probably sounded absurdly jubilant.

He said, "Yes, I know," in a patient way that took the wind out of my sails. He went on, "We have just heard. Her mother is being informed." He sounded very cold and unmoved about the whole thing and although I knew that it was unreasonable to expect anything else I felt childishly angry.

I said, hoping I suppose to excite some feeling in him, "She is very ill."

He sounded almost amused. "We hope she will recover. For our sake if not for her own, poor girl."

The compassion was perfunctory. I might have asked him what he meant if I had not thought, suddenly, about Humphrey and what Rose's testimony might mean to him. I said good-bye to Jennings and sat for a long time in the bright box, staring at the telephone. There began to grow, in my mind, a small and terrifying doubt.

Chapter Twelve

Rose did not die. It was three days before they were sure she would live and for three days I thought of no one else. I spent as much time as I could at my club drinking whisky in the bar and waiting for a telephone call to say that she was dead. I slept very little and I barely spoke to anyone. I behaved, I suppose, like a middle-aged fool.

Mrs. Blacker came to London. I found her a quiet hotel in a back street and met her at the station and took her there. She was wearing her brown hat and coat and shiny, pointed shoes. She cried a great deal, although whether she cried for herself or for Rose, I did not know. She sat by Rose's bed in the hospital for a large part of each day and the nurses brought her cups of tea. I don't think she realised why the policeman stayed with Rose. She did not mention his presence to me and the nurses in the ward said that she behaved, all the time, as if he were not there.

On the fourth day Rose made a statement to the police. We were quite a social gathering round her bed—Jennings, a police sergeant, a nurse and a doctor.

Rose sat up in the hard high bed and she looked very fragile and pretty. Pallor suited her; it threw into relief the astonishing dark beauty of her eyes and the curves of her mouth. The nurse had tied a bright ribbon round her hair and she looked pleased and excited like a child at a treat. I thought that she did not quite realise what was going on and it made me feel tender and protective.

At first Jennings was very gentle with her. He sat on the end of the bed and talked to her in a kindly, unofficial way. He called her "my dear" and said that she mustn't worry. He asked her about

Jasmine Castle and she said that she had known her since they had been at school together. After Jasmine had left they had written, to one another. Then, when she had gone to London they had gone out together. They had gone quite often to The Odd Flamingo. Jasmine knew some boys who went there and the boys had taken them out and given them a good time.

She said anxiously, "There wasn't anything wrong in that, was there? I never went out with boys at home. Mummy thought I was too young. She didn't understand that I wanted some fun. It's only natural, isn't it? I mean, for a girl to want some fun?"

Her eyes were fixed on the policeman who was taking down notes in shorthand. He gave her a quick look and went on writing and the back of his neck was scarlet. He was a very young policeman and impressionable. She smiled as though she were innocently pleased at the effect she had made.

She went on, "I didn't tell Mummy about Jasmine because I thought she'd be angry if she knew we'd been to a club and had some drinks. She's teetotal, you see."

Jennings said, "Were you friendly with any particular boy?" He wasn't looking at Rose. He had taken a paper knife out of his pocket and was playing with it in an absent-minded way. It was a pretty thing with a carved ivory handle.

She said, "Oh, yes. But we were just friends. I mean—Jimmie was in love with me but I thought of him as just a friend. Then when I got ill that evening, he took me down to the river in a car and let me stay in, his boat. It was ever so nice of him and I hope he won't get into trouble. He won't, will he?"

Jennings said, "Why didn't you let your mother know you were ill?"

She seemed, suddenly, unsure of herself; she began to cough and held her side as though it hurt her. Then she said, "I was so terribly ill. I wanted to die. I thought Jimmie would let her know. Didn't he tell her?"

Jennings said, "Do you know that Jasmine Castle is dead?" He was still speaking quietly but there was no longer any gentleness in his voice. He looked at Rose with an air of bright enquiry, his good ear bent towards her.

She didn't look like a child at a party now. She shrank back into the pillows, her mouth quivering as if she were going to cry.

She said, "No. No." And then she cried out, ill fear, "I don't remember anything. Anything at all. Why is she dead? What happened to her?"

The doctor went to the head of the bed and took her wrist in a professional way. He held it for a moment and then replaced it gently on the cover.

Jennings said, "Jasmine Castle was murdered." His voice was completely unemotional. He went on, "Will you tell us what happened on the evening of the ninth of August? You were with her, weren't you?"

She stared at him. Then she said, "It's all like some horrible dream. I can't bear to think about it."

"Try to tell us, won't you?" Jennings said. The young policeman was gazing fixedly at his notebook as if he wasn't liking his job very much. I couldn't look at Rose any longer so I stared at the shadows on the white wall behind her bed. The shadow of Jennings's head was long and narrow, little spiky tufts stuck out from the back of his head where the hair would not lie down.

Her voice was stumbling and soft. She said, "My head is so muddled. I'll try not to get it wrong. I was going to meet a gentleman friend that evening but I didn't want to. So Jasmine said that we'd see him together and tell him that we were going somewhere else. I didn't want to see him at all but she said that we ought to."

"Was this man, the one you were going to see, Mr. Humphrey Stone?"

She said, "Yes, it was Mr. Stone."

"Did your friend know him?"

"I think so. He used to go to the Flamingo."

"Had you talked to Jasmine Castle about your own relationship with Mr. Stone?"

She said, "I don't know. I think I did. Oh, my head does hurt so. Why are you asking me all these questions?" She began to whimper quietly; she looked very forlorn. I felt righteously and ridiculously angry. She was sick and frightened; it was wrong that she should be tormented like this.

Jennings said stolidly, "Please tell me what happened that evening, Miss Blacker."

She stopped crying and looked at him with wide, blank eyes. Her words were stilted. "We met Mr. Stone in the street. He took us to a pub. I didn't really want anything to drink but he made me have one and I didn't want to make a fuss and say no. Then we all talked for a bit. He was ever so upset because I couldn't have dinner with him and he said couldn't he meet us later when we had finished with our date? I didn't want to. Jasmine did. She kept on at me to say I'd go, but I wouldn't. So he didn't fix anything up, not while I was there, anyway."

"What do you mean?"

"Well—really—I wasn't there all the time. I had to go to the toilet."

"Did they say any more about meeting after you got back?"

"Not exactly. After Mr. Stone had gone, Jasmine said that I was mean and spoiled all her fun. I said she knew why I didn't want to see Mr. Stone any more. Anyway we were going to see the boys. She said of course we were going to see the boys but we didn't have to stay with them for the rest of the evening."

Jennings said, "Why didn't you want to see Mr. Stone, Miss Blacker?"

She put her hands up to her face and then she took them away and looked straight at Jennings and said, "I was going to have a baby. You know that, don't you? It's why I was so ill. It was Mr. Stone's baby."

He said, "Are you quite sure about that?"

Her eyes were very bright and there was the brittle smile on her mouth that I remembered from our first meeting. There was a soft, shy tremor in her voice. She said, "I'm quite sure about it. He was in love with me. I know it was wrong, doing what I did, but he was ever so much in love with me. Just like on the films. At least, he said he was in love with me and I thought he meant it. Afterwards I wasn't sure."

Her voice shook a little but she went on almost defiantly, "That was when I told him about the baby. He said it wasn't his baby. I couldn't understand what had happened. He was quite different—sort of cold and hard. It broke my heart, really it did."

Jennings said, "And what about the man Callaghan?"

"I told you, he was just a friend. He wanted me to marry him but I couldn't do that. It wouldn't have been right, would it? He was ever so angry when I told him about the baby and ever so upset. It was natural with him being in love with me like he was." She sounded pathetically proud that Jimmie had been in love with her.

Jennings asked her what had happened after they had left Humphrey on the ninth of August.

She said, "We went to the Flamingo but only Jimmie was there. It was ever so hot and noisy at the club so we thought we'd go for a drive. Jimmie had a smashing new car with an open top and it was lovely and cool. I sat in the front with Jimmie and Jasmine sat in the back. I think she felt a bit out of it with Jimmie feeling about me the way he did. She used to go with him, you see. After a bit she got cross and said it wasn't any fun and couldn't we go somewhere exciting? I had an awful pain in my inside and I felt awfully sick so I said I thought I'd rather just sit in the car as it was so hot. So she told Jimmie to stop the car and she got out in an awful temper and went away."

"Did she say where she was going?"

She shook her head. She seemed, suddenly to be completely without confidence. There was something almost desperate in her face and manner.

"What happened then, Miss Blacker?"

She said, "The pain got worse. It was awful. Jimmie was ever so nice to me and he said he'd take me home but I didn't want to go. My auntie doesn't like me. I thought the pain might be something to do with the baby and I was afraid of her knowing about it. So Jimmie said he'd take me to his boat and I could be quiet there and lie down and perhaps the pain would go. But it didn't go. When I got to the boat it was so awful that I wanted to die. I made Jimmie stay with me for a little while but he got frightened and said he would get someone else. He asked a woman he knew to come and see me and she said that I ought to go to hospital but I cried and cried and in the end she said that perhaps it would be all right and I could stay in the boat. Then it got worse and my head ached and it hurt when I breathed. I don't remember anything after that. Don't ask me any more, please don't ask me any more."

The tears were running down her face. She looked pitiable. The young sergeant was bright pink and he muttered under his breath.

Jennings said, "Miss Blacker, did you know that your friend, Jasmine Castle, was blackmailing Mr. Stone?"

She looked at him with wide, shocked eyes. Then she moaned and fell back against the supporting pillows with her eyes closed. The doctor and the nurse went up to her and bent over the bed. Then the doctor turned round to us and said, "I think she's had enough."

She came round quite quickly and by the time we left she was crying quietly and drearily with the nurse's arm round her shoulders.

We left the hospital together, Jennings walking neatly beside me, his police sergeant a few steps behind.

As we reached the street he said, in a tired way, "She was lying, of course. They all lie." He stopped and looked pensively at the pavement. "In my job you see so many of these girls. Some of them are bad, most of them are silly. And most of them lie."

I said, angry with him and ashamed because I was showing it, "I thought she was telling the truth."

He said, "Maybe she was," and shrugged his shoulders. "But she went with a nasty crowd. It's hard to believe she didn't know about them. You can't touch pitch and not be defiled."

He spoke complacently as if he had thought of the phrase himself.

I said, uncomfortably because it was a difficult thing to say, "I think it would be possible—for real innocence."

He turned and looked at me and his eyes had no expression in them at all. They were like pieces of opaque glass. He said, "She's badly scared, isn't she?" And then, looking away from me, "You know, if she's telling the truth, it looks bad for Mr. Stone."

Mrs. Blacker was waiting for me in the lounge of her hotel. She had ordered tea and we sat in immense and stuffy armchairs and ate refined sandwiches made of shrimp-and-salmon paste. I told her what Rose had said.

She put her cup back in its saucer and placed it carefully on the table. Her colourless eyes were hard and she spoke with satisfied anger.

"She's made it sound as if it wasn't really her fault, hasn't she? It's just like her. She can wriggle out of anything, or thinks she can. She's been like that ever since she was a little girl. When she was naughty she always managed to make it look as if she hadn't been. She'd look at you with those big black eyes and say, `But Mummy, I didn't *mean* to be naughty.' I suppose she thinks that now she isn't going to have a baby it will all be forgotten and forgiven. Well, it won't be. I know all about her now. I won't be taken in by her baby face and fancy ways. She's a bad, wicked girl and I'm not going to let her forget it."

I said, "Mrs. Blacker, she's been very ill. You mustn't be too hard on her."

She licked her lips with her tongue in a nervous, excited way. She said, "And how about me, Mr. Hunt? It's not going to be easy for me with all the neighbours knowing she's been mixed up with the police and whispering about it behind my back. It's not nice, you know, to go down to the shops and find people talking when you come near them and looking at you in a funny sort of way so that you know they've been talking about you. I go cold all over when I think of it; I wake up in the night thinking of it and I can't go to sleep again. I suppose I thought too much of her, more than I ought to have done, and God has punished me for it."

I said clumsily, "You mustn't feel like that." She said, "I don't know, I'm sure," and the empty little phrase carried a burden of desolation so that I felt anger die away in a kind of useless pity for this shabby, skinny woman for whom the summit of shame and horror was her neighbours' gossiping.

As I came away I knew that what she and Jennings thought about Rose was what everyone would think about her. I wished, desperately, that I could stand between her and the world's easy judgment. And I knew that there was nothing that I could do.

It was early evening and it was beginning to be cold. I went back to my club and had dinner. By the time. I came out into the streets again it was almost dark. I went to the hospital to ask about Rose. The night staff had come on duty and the sister did not know me. At first she refused to let me see Rose; after I had argued for a bit she said, reluctantly, that she would telephone Matron and went into the office to do so leaving me outside in the entrance to the ward. I waited there for a little time, staring at the bare walls and feeling stifled by the scent of the flowers that had been brought out of the ward for the night and stood on the floor in neat rows outside the sluice.

The night sister came back angry and ruffled. She said, crossly, that I could see Rose and speak to her if she was awake. But I was not to wake her up and that I was to remember that she had been ill.

I felt like a tiresome small boy. She escorted me to the door of Rose's room and left me there.

There was a light burning above the bed. Rose was propped against the pillows but her head had fallen sideways and she was asleep. Her mouth was a little open and the skin of her forehead glistened with a faint, damp sheen. With her eyes closed her prettiness was rather ordinary and she looked extremely vulnerable. She twitched in her sleep and moaned. I stood at the end of the bed and watched her.

I thought, once or twice, that she was on the point of waking. She rolled her head restlessly on the pillows and it slipped even further sideways, coming up with a sharp jerk that I thought must wake her. But each time this happened she sighed and went on sleeping.

Then she cried in her sleep, softly and with a sharp note of alarm, so that when she opened her eyes I was not surprised to see them quite senseless with terror, staring and very bright.

She saw me at the end of the bed and for a moment she watched me without comprehension. I was afraid she would cry out; I went close to her and bent over the bed.

I said, "It's all right, Rose. You're all right now."

The little room was not completely separated from the rest of the ward; the partitions did not go all the way up to the ceiling, so that I could hear the other patients moving and muttering in their beds. If we talked too loudly we would be heard and one of the nurses would come.

She said, "What do you want? It's night-time."

I said, "It's all right. I want to ask you something. Did you have a bad dream? Has something frightened you?"

She said nothing, her black eyes were fixed on my face.

I said gently, "I won't hurt you, Rose. What are you afraid of? No one can hurt you here."

The sweat ran in glistening threads down her face. Her hands groped separately across the counterpane and clasped together until the knuckles went white.

I searched in my mind for the tiny thing that had perplexed me. "Rose, who was the poor old man? What happened to him?"

She made a low, shapeless sound like a hurt animal and cowered back into the pillows.

I said, "What happened to Jasmine? Do you know?"

She moved her head from side to side on the pillows. She made no further sound.

I said, "Is it anything to do with Piers Stone? You both knew him, didn't you? Why did Jasmine have your handbag?"

She said, "She took it when she ran away. They were the same, hers and mine."

I said, "Why did she run away?"

She said desperately, "Go away. I don't know. I don't know."

I said, "Rose, if you were afraid of something that might happen to you in London, why did you go back? You didn't have to, did you?"

She said, "Jasmine made me. I had to. They'll get me if I tell." There was a sudden gleam in her eyes and she said more coherently, "I'm ill. I don't know what I'm saying."

She was speaking more loudly and I glanced over my shoulder. I could hear someone coming down the ward with the flat, clumping steps of a woman in low-heeled shoes.

I said, "Rose, it's important. You must tell me what happened. I won't let them hurt you. Can't you trust me?"

I longed for her to trust me, for her to let me enclose her with protection and love. But she began to cry weakly, putting her arm across her eyes. It was a young, thin arm, the skin stretched tautly from the elbow to the arm pit and the bones stood out sharply.

I said, "Rose, dear Rose, don't cry. Tell me about the bad dream. About the poor old man."

She screamed at the top of her lungs. The partition door jerked open and a nurse ran to the head of the bed. She was a probationer, even younger than Rose, and her round face gleamed with health and honest anger.

She wrapped protective arms round Rose. She said, "Sister says you must go." And she turned to Rose and held the dark head to her apron front.

She said, in a soft croon, "There, there. It's all right. You're all right now."

Across the bent, black head she looked indignantly at me and I felt both shame and a desire to vindicate myself before her clear-eyed anger.

I said, "I'm sorry. I didn't want to upset her. But it was important."

The girl blushed brightly as though it were a great effort not to say a great many things that she would have liked to say. In the silence her eyes said them for her. I felt that I had had the worst of it.

I left the little room and closed the door gently behind me. I could hear the nurse's voice muffled through the door, talking in a gentle sing-song. The night sister was in her office as I went past and she must have heard me but she did not look up.

When I went out into the night it was dark and still; the starless sky pressed heavily down over London.

I think it was chance that took me to the Sandown Road; I did not, in fact, realise where I was until I was near the end of the road and saw the wooden fence that bordered the canal and the black sky above. The street was busier than most streets at this time; it wasn't until I saw the women standing singly in the shadows of the tall houses that I realised why.

And then I heard a woman scream. The scream came from high up in one of the old houses. I stopped the car and switched off the ignition. The screaming went on in a shrill, regular fashion like a steam engine. I got half out of the car and stood with one foot on the running board. At that point the screaming stopped abruptly.

One of the women moved out of the shadows and up to the car.

I said, uneasily, "Oughtn't we to do something? Is there anything wrong, do you think?"

The woman chuckled. "Lor bless you, no," she said. "That'd be trespass. You don't go interferin' round here, you know. You wouldn't 'alf cop it if you did."

She paused a moment and added a professional enquiry. I said that I was in a hurry just now.

She chuckled again in a nice way and said, "No offence taken, I'm sure." She seemed to be in an excellent temper.

I got back into the car and drove away. No one seemed to have taken any notice of the screaming; I wondered, abstractedly, whether it was always the same in that kind of street.

Chapter Thirteen

Jennings said, "He was arrested early this morning. In London. He will be charged with the murder."

His face was scarred like a nut. The room was full of sunlight like yellow water; it shone on Jennings, small and dusty behind his big official desk.

I had known all along that it was inevitable; knowledge did not lessen the shock, the physical numbing of despair.

I said, "How did you find him?"

"He went to his brother's flat. His brother told us he was there."

I said, "Piers?" and Jennings nodded. I stared at him and he blushed slowly as if he was embarrassed on my behalf, his skin turning a brownish red.

I banged my pipe out on the sill of the opened window. Outside there was a flurried sky and the first leaves were falling gustily from the tall plane trees.

Then I told him about Piers and The Odd Flamingo and the drugs. He listened to me, his face as blank as a piece of clean paper.

He said, "Yes, we know. We've known about it for some time. We were waiting for more information."

"You don't think it had anything to do with the murder?"

He said, "Why should it? As far as we know, the girl knew nothing. Wherever you look in that sort of society you find some kind of dirty business. It doesn't follow that it has any relevance."

He shrugged his shoulders in weary acceptance of expected evil; his eyes looked sad as if he were sorry for me.

I asked him about the old man called Menhennet and I told him about Rose's nightmare.

He nodded. "We know about that, too," he said. He sounded tired and omniscient. "He was killed. Robbery with violence. We didn't get anyone for it. It was small fry; it had that kind of mark on it. A bungled business."

I said, "How did he die?"

"He was old. They gagged him and tied him up and he died, in the end, of shock. He shouldn't have been at home at that time of the day—he had some kind of a job at the council offices. So it is unlikely that his murder was intended. That morning he hadn't been well and he'd stayed at home. He was something of a miser and he'd talked about it. He kept about thirty pounds in a jar on the mantelpiece and it was gone. He lived with a niece; she said he didn't trust the post office."

I said, "Why should Rose be so frightened about it?"

I thought that he looked wary suddenly. He played with his paper knife without looking at me and then he said, "It was a frightening way to die, wasn't it?" His voice trailed off into silence; he dug at the blotting paper before him with the blunt point of the knife.

I saw Humphrey at the police station, briefly, and with a policeman in attendance. The days he had been on the run had completed his disintegration; he was, now, an exhausted, shambling man with a look in his eyes that was a little mad. Even his anger added nothing to his stature. It was natural that he should be obsessed with the sense of injustice done to him, but somehow he turned a show of innocence and indignation into petulance and whining. I felt stifled all the time I was with him and I was glad to come away. I was ashamed because I felt like that. It was a kind of betrayal.

The Ealing street was comfortable and middle-class with detached, double-fronted houses that had no architectural merit but looked solid and permanent and sound. The years and the inclination of the inhabitants had grown high hedges and thick shrubberies around each house, so that when I opened the gate and walked into the gravelled drive I knew that I could not be seen from the neighbouring windows through the screen of laurels and damp yews.

There was a board displayed on the front porch that said the house was for sale and gave the address of the local estate agents.

The woman who opened the door was perhaps in her late forties. She was stout and neat and indeterminate in feature so that afterwards I was unable to remember what she looked like. She was drab and uniformly grey.

She said, without interest, "Have you come about the house?" and I was glad that she had given me such an easy and obvious excuse.

I nodded, adding, in case there should be trouble later, that I had not been to the agents but that someone had told me about the house and that, as I was passing, I had hoped that someone might be in.

She said ungraciously, "Well, you'd better come in as you're here."

I went into the hall. She showed me over the house without, apparently, feeling any curiosity about me or indeed, any particular interest in the house itself. It was a dull house with a great deal of dull furniture in it; it was as insignificant as the woman herself so that by the time we had looked into every room and into every cupboard I felt a kind of despair at the thought that people should live in it.

We went into the drawing-room. It was comfortable and dreary and little used. The chairs and the carpet were fairly new and looked expensive.

She said, "Of course, I wouldn't be selling, only I'd like a smaller place. It's too much for one and I'm out all day. I thought of a nice flat—no stairs to clean, you see. Somewhere central and nice and bright."

She looked round the room we stood in with a groping puzzlement as though she knew there was something wrong about it and was not sure what it was.

I said, uncomfortably, "Yes, it's a big house for one person, alone."

"Of course I haven't been alone till now," she said. "When my husband was killed—he was a warden and a bomb destroyed the post when he was on duty—my uncle came and lived with me. He used to live in Chelsea but he was too old to be on his own in London. He'd had a stroke some years back, you see. He passed on a few months ago and since then I've been thinking about selling the house. All my friends said I was silly to stay here but I didn't make up my mind, really, until a couple of weeks ago."

She gave me a sudden, sly look as if she were wondering how much I knew.

I said, "I read about your uncle in the papers. It must have been a shock to you."

She flushed and said, "Oh—then you *do* know? My friends said that it might make it difficult to sell the house. People are funny about that sort of thing, aren't they? I mean, don't you think some people might be put off, knowing what had happened?"

I said, "It wouldn't worry me. But it must have been very distressing for you."

"Oh. Yes, it was." She stared at the floor and then she said, with a sudden glow of excitement, "You know, it happened here, right in this room. I found him when I came home from the office. I was late—we'd been stocktaking—and it was getting dark. I'd had a bite to eat with my friends in town and it must have been about ten o'clock. I thought it was funny that there wasn't a light and then I thought perhaps he'd gone to the club. A nasty place that he used to go to in the Fulham Road. Not that he spent any money there—a real old skinflint he was, though I suppose I shouldn't speak ill of the dead. He never paid me a penny for his board and lodging all the time he was here and he liked his comforts, I can tell you. My friends said they didn't know how I put up with him. He saved every penny of what he earned—not that it was much, mind you, but he had his pension as well. He used to keep some of it on the mantelpiece—about thirty pounds he had there, I think. He kept it in other places in the house too but *they* didn't get the rest of it because he'd hidden it too well. Up in the loft, mostly, and sewn into his mattress. The trouble I had finding it all, you wouldn't believe! And there's still some of it left, I shouldn't wonder. I used to tell him we'd be murdered in our beds and he used to laugh at me. Well, I was right, wasn't I? That's the first thing I thought when I saw him lying on that sofa there, stiff as a board. Tied up like a sack, he was, with his head hanging over the end. Of course I was properly upset; my nerves haven't been the same since it happened. They got away with about thirty pounds. It's a mercy it wasn't more."

It wasn't really that she was hard, I think; merely mercenary and quite unself-conscious about it. I wondered if, in the beginning, she had made any attempt at grief.

I said, "Did many people know about the money? Did he talk about it?"

"Oh yes, he talked about it all right. Though whether he was believed is another matter. He hadn't one good suit. I can tell you, I used to be ashamed for people to know he was my uncle. But it wasn't my place to buy clothes for him when he had all that money, now was it? He was just an old miser, almost like something in a book."

"Had you told anyone locally about the money?"

"I don't know many people here now. It's working in London, you see, and besides all my friends have moved away. It used to be a really nice district before the war; ever such nice people used to live in this road but it has gone down since then. Of course I know my neighbours in a manner of speaking, but they're not the sort of people I'd like to make friends with."

I said, "Then someone must have listened to your uncle. When he boasted about his money."

"Oh," she said, "I don't think anyone would listen to *him*. He was an old fool. Everyone used, to laugh at him—the people at his club and all. He used to get really nasty about it sometimes—he'd come home here in ever such a temper and say he'd show them he wasn't going to be treated like that. He used to talk about something that he was going to tell to the police—just a lot of foolishness, of course, and I never paid any heed to it. Nor would anyone in their senses."

I said, "Then how did they know about the money?"

"I don't know," she said. "There was the girl, of course. The police wanted to know a lot about her—there was a man here only yesterday—but I don't think she can have had anything to do with it. Ever such a nice girl, she was, nicely spoken. A good-class sort of girl."

I asked, "Why did she come?" and she gave me a sudden, suspicious look, a glance that was both mean and cunning, but then her face assumed its ordinary blankness and she told me about it.

The girl had come on a Saturday morning about two weeks before old Menhennet had been killed. She had stood in the front porch with a timid, frightened air, facing the door but with her body half-turned towards the gate as if she were ready to run away. Her manner gave credibility to her story; it was shy and faltering as if she were indeed, as she said, homeless and looking for shelter. She had come, she said, because someone had told her there was a room to let in the house. This was, in a way, true; the woman had been thinking of taking a lodger and she had mentioned her intention to several people locally although she had, by this time, decided against doing so. But for some reason she did not say so at once, something both desperate and forlorn in the girl's appearance sharpened her curiosity and she asked her to come in.

When the door was closed and they stood together in the dark hall the girl said, "I must have somewhere to go. There's nowhere. I can't go home."

She seemed on the verge of tears and exhaustion and the woman, who was already regretting bringing her into the house, offered her, grudgingly, a cup of tea.

While she drank the tea the girl said, "You will think me a dreadful person, coming into your house like this. I wouldn't have come, but what else could I do? *She* said I was to get out and not to come back again. She threw a saucepan at me."

She had rolled up the sleeve of her light dress and shown a dark, purpling bruise on the delicate arm.

The woman asked her what had happened and the girl hesitated. Then she said, "I mustn't trouble you, really. It's my worry, not yours." But she went on, "I must tell someone. It's all bottled up inside me—do you mind? You see, my mother hates me. That sounds silly, doesn't it? But it's true. She's jealous of me because I'm young and she's not and because my father and I are such good friends. We've always loved each other in rather a special way. Daddy has been out East for most of his life, you see, and when I was younger I used to be with him. My mother stayed in England a lot—she used to say the climate didn't suit her although I don't think that was true. Then, when Daddy retired and came home she didn't like the way we were so fond of each other. She'd got to look a lot older and she'd started to drink a lot. It was awful. She'd get drunk and then she'd come into the room where Daddy and I were sitting and make a terrible scene. She didn't like us being together at all—she was always on at me to go out and find some friends of my own. Then, this morning, she screamed at me because I was late for breakfast. She told me to get out and she threw a saucepan at me and hit me. She smelt of whisky—it was horrible. I didn't mind what she did to me, if *he'd* wanted me to stay I'd have put up with anything. But he was in the room when it happened and when he went out without saying anything and looking sort of beaten and tired, I knew I couldn't stay any more. So I packed a case and came away. I've been walking about all day looking for somewhere to go."

She put her head down on the table and burst into violent, shaking sobs.

The woman had listened eagerly; the girl's beauty and her rôle of victim excited her. She comforted her a little and then she capped the girl's story with confidences of her own. She didn't say how much she had said but I guessed, from her half-ashamed admissions that she had, in fact, produced a hard-luck story about the maddening old uncle who clung so persistently and so meanly to a life that was no longer of any use to him. And clung, which was more important, to his money too. She admitted reluctantly that she had told the girl about the money. She was not willing to be too precise about what she had said; she was aware, it seemed, of her own stupidity. She said that the girl had been sympathetic; they had talked a little longer and then she had offered her a temporary lodging until she could find somewhere else.

"It was the least I could do, wasn't it? I mean she seemed so genuine and I didn't like to turn her away. She seemed very grateful and then she said she would go down to the station and get her bag."

She reddened, slowly and hideously, "She didn't come back," she said.

"What was she like?" I asked.

She wrinkled her forehead. "The police wanted to know that, too. She was very pretty and nicely dressed. Good taste, you know, nothing cheap or showy. She had glasses on and her hair was tied back with a ribbon." She looked at me suspiciously. "You're very interested in her, aren't you?"

I said quickly, "Yes. I've not told you the truth, I'm afraid. I don't want the house. I wanted to know about the girl."

She took that quite calmly. "If she did have something to do with it, shall I get the money back?"

She leaned forward and moistened her lips with her tongue and suddenly I was very conscious of the hot, musty smell in the room and of a deep, almost physical distaste.

I said, "I don't know. I'm not from the police. But I shall tell them about this. And I dare say they'll get in touch with you."

She nodded and smiled suddenly in a coy, unattractive way. "Well, you're a funny one, aren't you? I never guessed. Oh, you're a deep one, all right."

I left the house with relief and a feeling of tiredness that was of the mind as well as of the body. I was most of the way through the wood and it gave me no feeling of achievement or exaltation whatever.

Menhennet had died by accident, but it was an accident that had led to another death. Jasmine could be trusted to keep her mouth shut about a robbery in which she had herself been concerned but murder was another matter. I wondered how often she had been used for this sort of thing and whether she had inherited her histrionic ability from her mother.

And Rose had an excellent reason to be afraid; an excellent reason to lie. Jasmine had told her about the old man, Menhennet, and Jasmine had been murdered. They had not killed Rose, because Callaghan loved her enough to hide her in his boat. But she was not hidden in his boat now. She was in the hands of the police and sooner or later she would tell them what she knew. Unless she were prevented from telling them. And there was only one way of preventing her.

I stopped the car and went into the telephone box outside. The door would not shut properly and the noise of the traffic dulled the ringing tone.

When the hospital answered I had difficulty, at first, in making out what they said. It was not entirely because of the traffic. I did not want to hear that Rose had been taken away by her mother.

I rang the hotel and Mrs. Blacker came to the telephone after some delay. She sounded peevish. Yes, she said, Rose was in her room. And in bed. Yes, she was quite all right, only a little tired and in need of sleep. The people in the hotel were being very kind; they had sent up her lunch on a tray. And a man had been in and left some flowers. He had asked to see Rose but she had sent a message and said it was impossible. No, she had not seen the man, she did not know his name. There had been no name on the card that came with the flowers, only the words, "With sympathy." She supposed the man had gone away.

I said, "Go back to Rose. Stay with her. Don't leave her."

She said, crossly, that of course she would stay with Rose, that she would not have left her now if I had not telephoned.

I put the receiver down and stood in the box wondering whether I should ring the police. Whether by the time I had made somebody understand it might not be too late.

Now that it was entirely my decision I felt inadequate and weak, afraid that behind my hesitation lay a fear of ridicule. I left the box and went back to the car.

I drove as fast as I could to the hotel. It was in a back street, a street so quiet that it might have been a street in a provincial town. The grey dust blew along it and there were torn papers in the gutters. A ginger torn slept on the hotel steps and the sleazy windows looked dead and still.

There was a long grey car parked almost opposite the hotel entrance on the far side of the road. It was a narrow road and it led into a T-junction that ran from a cul-de-sac in a yard behind an office block into the main street. I managed to get past the grey car, putting my wheels up on to the kerb in front of the hotel and swinging in front of the bonnet of the other car. I switched off the ignition and got out of my seat.

Through the windscreen of the other car I saw Piers's face. It was white and blubbery and shocked. I went up to the car and put my hand on the open window. Piers struck at my knuckles with a sudden and violent gesture and the sharp edge of the window jarred into my finger joints. I drew back in anger and alarm and said his name aloud.

Piers blew a long, loud blast on the horn.

After that it all seemed to happen at once. The shot from the hotel and the loud, high scream and the sudden filling of the little, quiet street with people.

The hotel door swung open and crashed back into the face of the porter who was glimpsed, momentarily, through the glass, his surprised and bloodied face sinking backwards out of sight.

The young man who came out wore a handkerchief covering the lower part of his face like a boy's conception of an American gangster. He had silken bleached hair that caught the summer sun. He looked at the car and at me and then he ran towards the T-junction and several uniformed police scuttled out of doorways and gave chase.

Piers swore, he slammed the car into gear and tried to swing the wheel but there wasn't enough room. He flung himself out of the car on the far side and ran, away from the hotel towards the busy shopping street. I dodged round the car and caught my foot in a drain-cover and fell. It only stopped me for a moment but it was long enough to give Piers, old and fat as he was, a start of almost the length of the street.

I am not sure why I ran after him; it would have been more sensible, in the end, to leave him to the police.

At the end of the quiet street the traffic streamed past; there was a lull as Piers reached the kerb and he ran across to the island in the centre of the road. Once there he was marooned; it was the city's lunch hour, the traffic was thick and there was no chance to cross.

I stood on the pavement watching him; the buses passed in an unbroken line and all the time Piers stood on the island, looking back at me.

When, finally, there was a gap and I slipped across the road in front of the bonnet of a lorry, we looked into each other's faces for perhaps thirty seconds and in that time I had my entire revenge for Humphrey and for Kate and for Rose.

His face was a mask of animal terror. He was sweating and the sweat ran into his eyes and trickled down his chin from the corners of the twisted mouth. His face was the colour of lard.

Then he lunged at me with his flabby fists raised above his head and his mouth open and shouting something that I could not hear. I side-stepped and he fell, forward into the road. I could not have saved him; I am quite sure that I could not have saved him.

As he went under the bus he screamed. He went on screaming long after it seemed incredible that he should not be dead, long after I had begun to pray that he would die soon.

Chapter Fourteen

At the time and afterwards it seemed as if the whole horrible business had lasted for hours; but in fact it could not have been more than a few minutes before the bus had stopped and the screaming had ended and the gasping, gawping crowd was so thick on the road and round the island that I had trouble getting out of it. I felt winded and sick. As I reached the pavement a man caught me by the arm and then, after a look at my face, let me go again. I think he shouted after me as I ran back along the street to the hotel.

The foyer was noisy and full of people. The porter was sitting on the floor with his back against the reception desk. Blood streamed down his face and he wore an expression of aggrieved astonishment. No one seemed to be taking any notice of him.

I ran up the stairs to the first floor. There were people in Mrs. Blacker's room and a bitter smell of smoke. Rose was half out of bed, crouching on her knees, her face empty and staring. Mrs. Blacker lay in a wicker chair and gasped like a fish. Her feet drummed faintly on the carpeted floor.

I went to Rose and said, "It's all right, my sweet, my dear. Lie down. You're all right now."

She looked at me as if she didn't know who I was. I took her by the shoulders and pushed her down under the bedclothes and she lay still, like an obedient child, her eyes fixed on my face.

The manager was by the bed, his poky, cockney face grey as ashes. I said, "Call the police. And get these people out of here."

He looked at mie with relief, not questioning my authority. He said, "Yes, sir. Of course, sir."

They were gone in a few minutes and the door was closed and there was no sound in the room except Mrs. Blacker's shuddering sobs. Then she stopped crying and her voice was harsh with shock, and trembly.

She said, "There was a man. He came in with a gun. He didn't say anything at all. I was at the window and when I looked round he was there. Then someone blew a horn and the gun went off. He ran away."

Rose said nothing. She turned her head on the pillow and looked at me with eyes that were enormous with terror. I sat beside her on the bed and took her cold hand in mine. I said, "Rose dear, it's all over. You won't have to be frightened again. I know about the old man. Will you tell me about him?"

She shook her head in a quick, convulsed gesture; she did not take her eyes from my face.

I said, "Jasmine knew all about it, didn't she? She went to Ealing?"

The door of the room opened and Jennings came in. He closed the door with the smallest sound and leant against it. He was breathing heavily as if he had been running.

I said, to Rose, "Was Jasmine there when the old man died."

There was a look of surprise on her face. Her eyes went past me, to Jennings. He walked to the end of the bed and his eyes were full of contempt and bitter anger.

"No," he said. "It wasn't Jasmine who was there. It was you, wasn't it?"

She nodded, or rather her head jerked forward as if she were a puppet and someone had pulled a string. She licked her lips with the tip of her pink tongue. Her eyes had a dulled, flat look.

For a moment I didn't know what was happening and then, when I did know, I wanted to get out of the room quickly before she was destroyed before my eyes. But it was too late; I had to stay and see it happen.

Jennings said, "Don't lie to me."

And she didn't lie. At least, not about what had happened. I had the feeling that although she twisted everything very slightly she was being, in her fashion, quite honest. She saw herself, genuinely, as wronged and essentially innocent. The distortion was deeply buried in her pitiable little mind and not deliberate. In the end I felt no anger with her, nor indignation, only pity.

She said, "Yes, I went there. I didn't know what they were going to do. Honestly I didn't. I just did what Jimmie wanted to do. Mr. Piers—he knew all about the old man and his money and he told Jimmie. I went down first to find out where he kept it. Then I went with Jimmie one morning and he broke into the house. I waited outside and Jimmie told me to tell him if anyone came. Then it all went wrong. The old man was in—he shouldn't have been in. The lady said he went out to work in the mornings. Jimmie came to the door and called me and told me to hurry. I went in and he'd got the old man on the floor and he held him while I tied his hands behind him. I didn't want to do it—he was such an old man and he looked all funny and blue round the mouth and he wasn't breathing properly. I said couldn't we just shut him up in a room, but Jimmie said no. He said he was a nark and that he knew who we were and that it wasn't safe. So we put him on a sofa and put a handkerchief in his mouth so he couldn't call out. Then Jimmie told me to go out and wait for him and I did and when he came out he was sick in the bushes. I didn't think he would die, truly I didn't. I didn't know he was dead until I read about it afterwards in the papers and then I was so afraid."

Jennings said, "And when you read about it in the papers, what did you do then?"

She did not take her eyes from his face. She said, "I was so frightened. I didn't know what to do. I wanted to get away—I didn't want to have anything to do with Jimmie any more. I'd not meant to do anything wrong, at first it had been just fun. Mr. Piers said you'd like some nice clothes, wouldn't you? And pretty things—I'd never had many pretty things, we'd always been too poor. And he said there was no harm in it if you were careful."

Jennings said, "What had Mr. Piers Stone to do with it all?"

She looked puzzled. "I'm not sure. Jimmie said he was a good sort, that he'd always say you were at the Flamingo if you didn't want people to know you'd been somewhere else. And he gave

Jimmie some stuff in a little packet. I don't know what it was but it was something awfully special and Jimmie said he'd let me have some of it one day if I was a good girl and did what I was told. Jimmie was terribly angry with Mr. Piers after Mr. Menhennet had died. He said he didn't see why he should do Mr. Stone's dirty work for him and that he didn't like people making a monkey out of him. I think Mr. Menhennet knew something about Mr. Stone that would have got him into trouble with the police."

Jennings said, each word a calculated drop of ice, "And when you found out that it wasn't just fun, that it was more dangerous than you thought, that you'd done something terrible, what did you do?"

Her mouth trembled and she said nothing.

He went on, "You were going to have Jimmie's baby, weren't you? And you thought that if you pretended it was someone else's baby Jimmie would have nothing more to do with you and you could break with him and the rest of the gang. The baby wasn't Mr. Stone's, was it?"

She shook her head dumbly.

"And then you found that it wasn't so easy. That they wouldn't let you go. You had a row with Callaghan and he threatened to kill you. That frightened you, didn't it? So you decided to go and see Mrs. Stone and tell her all about her husband and yourself. But it didn't work, did it?"

She said, in a small, still voice, "It was dreadfully wrong. But I didn't know what to do. Jimmie wanted me to marry him. Then, when I read in the papers that the old man was dead, I didn't want to have anything more to do with Jimmie. I hadn't wanted the old man to die—I hadn't wanted to tie him up. So it wasn't really my fault, was it?

"So I told Jimmie that I wouldn't marry him because I was going to have a baby and it wasn't his. He didn't believe me. So I had to make him believe me. I had all the letters Mr. Stone had written to me and I thought everyone would believe the baby was his. If I went to court, you see, it would all be public and Jimmie would have to believe me and leave me alone. And it wasn't just that I wanted him to leave me alone. It made me safer too. Because if I'd had the baby and hadn't said whose it was, people might have suspected about me and Jimmie. But if I said it was Mr. Stone's, then they wouldn't look for anyone else. I was so afraid, really I was. I didn't know what to do."

I felt ill with horror and disgust. I tried to hide it because I could see Jennings looking at me and I knew that he was sorry about it all.

Then he said, "And what happened on the night that Jasmine was killed?"

She looked round the room wildly, as if for help. She looked at Jennings and at me and at her mother. And then a change came over her face. It lost the crumpled lines of fear and became smoothly and almost horribly innocent. She looked quite astonishingly beautiful and curiously unreal. She lifted her head and smiled carefully at us all. It was a slow, sweet smile. She had escaped from her brief moment of reality; she was Joan of Arc at the stake.

She said, "I suppose it was all dreadfully wrong. But at first it seemed just exciting and not wrong at all. And you see"—wistfully—"life hasn't been very exciting for me. It's not much fun being shut up in a dull little town where no one wants you to enjoy yourself and everyone is jealous of you."

Then she spoke again of her fear when the old man had died. That it had been genuine fear, I did not doubt; that she had felt the smallest remorse was impossible to believe. I think the fact of the man's murder was still not quite real to her; once she spoke, almost petulantly, of their "bad luck" as if it had, in fact, seemed no more to her than that.

But she had been sufficiently afraid to want to break with Callaghan. He had attacked her. She put her little hands to her throat.

"I thought he would kill me," she said. "He was so strong. But the landlady stopped him. There were terrible bruises on my throat and on my arms. I thought I should die."

Jennings said, "But you saw him again, didn't you?"

Her eyes were clear and wide and young. "Yes," she said. "I had to see him."

I said suddenly, because I had to know, "But why? If you were so afraid of him, why did you go back to London?"

Her thin hands moved to her face and dropped away. Her white arms lay still on the bed cover. She said, "Jasmine made me. She made me come to London."

I think, even then, that she would have tried to keep back the worst and final guilt. If indeed she thought of it as guilt. But the silence in the room was waiting for her.

She said, "I told her about Mr. Menhennet. I thought she'd help me. But she didn't. She said it was a terrible thing to have done and that she ought to go to the police. I begged her not to do that and she said she wouldn't if I gave her money. I gave her what I had. Then she wrote to me and said she wanted twenty-five pounds. I hadn't got it and when I told her so she wrote to me again and said I must come to London and ask Jimmie for it. She said he'd have to give it to me. Then, when I came to London, I said that I couldn't see him alone and that she must come with me."

Jennings said, "But that was dangerous. Did you know how dangerous it would be for her?"

There was a terrible blankness in her face. "I thought that Jimmie would know what to do about her," she said.

It was, suddenly, quite cold in the room. Even Jennings looked shocked and still. I think that although he knew a great deal about ordinary evil he had not expected anything like this.

He said, in a dead voice, "But before you went to see Callaghan, you met Humphrey Stone?"

"Yes," she said, "we met Mr. Stone. I thought that if I could see him alone he might give me the money for Jasmine. I didn't really want Jimmie to hurt her. But I couldn't see him alone. Jasmine was there all the time."

"And so you went to see Callaghan?"

She nodded. Her face was still and cold so that the life and the loveliness were driven out of it. For a little while she did not speak and there was silence in the stuffy room that was only broken by the tapping of a torn blind against the half-opened window.

The blind went on tapping all the time that she was talking. I was aware of it constantly while I listened to the sharp little voice and its tale of betrayal and dismay.

She had expected to find Callaghan alone; but when they opened his door, Piers was there. He was sitting in a wicker chair by the window and when the two girls came in he stared at them hard with his bright, boot-button eyes and said nothing.

At first she said nothing about Jasmine or why she had brought her there. She had wanted to make her own position quite clear. This was to be a final meeting. She had prepared a set little speech. It was a novelettish affair intended to be very brave and very final. As they allowed her to speak, in silence, she gained in confidence and lost a little of her fear. Neither Piers nor the boy said anything while she produced her empty, careful little phrases about it all being for the best in the long run. Piers smiled gently in his wicker chair and Jimmie stood, with his back to the window, watching her. She did not look at him; she was afraid of the expression on his face.

When she had said all that she had intended to say there was a long silence so that she became uneasy and unsure.

At last Piers said, "That was very nicely said, Rose dear. Quite extraordinarily affecting. So there are to be no hard feelings between us then? I didn't know you were such a clever little actress. But there! Of course I knew. Jimmie told me how cleverly you behaved at Ealing. Why don't you both sit down?"

He smiled at the girls as if he found them very funny and they sat together on the hard divan bed.

Piers got up from his wicker chair and stood with his legs astride. He said, "We enjoyed listening to her, didn't we, James? But it isn't any good, my dear. How could James let you go? Think of how unhappy you have made him, dear. Have you the heart to leave him now?"

The gentle voice hardened and became immensely threatening.

He came across the room and stood above her, his eyes like small, wicked stones.

He said, "Rose, my dear, we can't let you go like this. You're too deeply in. It wouldn't be safe, now would it?"

Even then Rose had been unable to believe that they meant her any real harm. She had lived for so long in a world of her own dreaming that it did not seem that this was any more than an extension of her fantasy.

Then she told them about Jasmine. Jasmine who sat beside her, plucking at the sleeve of her coat with light, desperate fingers. Jasmine, who had been so completely without fear that she had not realised until now the extent of her own danger. It must have been a moment of extraordinary revelation and terror for her.

If anyone spoke, Rose did not remember what they said. She was only conscious of Piers's face coming closer and closer; of the wet mouth and the brilliant eyes. Then came the blow that knocked her, screaming, across the divan bed. For the moment the force of the impact drove the breath from her body, but when the moment had passed she screamed again with the full power of her young lungs until they held a cushion over her face. She could have screamed longer and louder in that neighbourhood and no one would have interfered.

She was aware that Jasmine had gone. The door banged and she heard Piers swearing. She was drowsy with shock and pain and she fainted.

When she came round again it was nearly dark in the room. There was a bundle of what tasted like wet flannel in her mouth and her lips felt stiff and bruised. They had gagged her roughly and tied her hands behind her back. Piers was in the room. He was smoking a cigar and the smell sickened her.

She stirred on the hard bed and he came over to her. He looked enormous and terrifying in the half dark.

Then the door opened and someone came in. Piers stood between the bed and the door; she did not know it was Jimmie until he said:

"I've done for her."

Piers moved away and she could see Jimmie's face. It was the colour of putty. He said, "She was screaming. She said she was going for the police. I had to shut the bitch's mouth. Didn't I? I had to do it."

His voice rose to a frightened shrillness. Piers went over to him and said something in a voice too low for Rose to hear. They both walked to the other end of the room, away from her.

They talked for a long time. Piers's voice was quick and angry. In the end he went away and she was alone with Jimmie. He came over to where she lay; his hair was lank with sweat and he breathed heavily into her face.

"Look here," he said. "I'll do you if you make a sound. Like I done the other bitch. You lay low and you'll be all right. See?"

He took the gag out of her mouth and unbound her hands and helped her to her feet. She was sick and dizzy but he made her button her coat and he picked up a white handbag from the floor and put it into her hand. They went out of the room and down the stairs to Jimmie's new car and she got in the seat beside him. They drove out of London; she did not dare to ask where they were going. She opened the handbag to make up her face and found that it was not her handbag, but Jasmine's. She did not tell him this; she was too afraid.

The pains began before they got to the boat. She was very sick. He helped her into the boat and on to the bunk and gave her water to drink. Then he went away and came back with a woman she had not seen before. After that she did not remember very much except that the woman was kind to her and helped her and when it was all over gave her some hot tea to drink which made her sick again.

Then she was better for a day or two; she lay in the hot bunk in the rocking boat and Jimmie brought her food and stayed with her sometimes. He had treated her gently. He told her that Jasmine was dead and that she must never tell anyone how it happened; that if she did they would arrest her and hang her. Slowly she began to realise the immensity of what she had done and her only fear became that they would find her and take her back. When she became ill again it was almost a relief. It would have been easier to die.

When she had finished no one spoke for a little while. Then Jennings went to the head of the bed and began to talk to her. He was impersonal and not at all unkind. She lay, an ashen little ghost in the untidy bed and the soft voice went on and on with a terrible and monotonous clarity.

They released Humphrey almost immediately and I did not see him again. He asked me to settle his affairs and gave me an address in Glasgow. After a while he sent for Celia and the boys. That was the end of it; I did not want to know what he was going to do. I felt only relief that I would not have to see him again.

They caught Jimmie Callaghan. He had hidden in a lodging house in the East End and when they came for him he got out through a back window. They ran him to ground in a blind alley at the back of the grey, slum houses. It was a wet night, the first of the wet, autumn nights, and dark. The boy hid among the dustbins and would not come out. He had a gun. One of the policemen went out into the open after him and Callaghan shot him through the head.

Then the fight was on. Jimmie Callaghan stood with his back against a wall and fired wildly at his inevitable end. He shouted all the time—disjointed, unreal sentences as if he saw himself, even now, as a character in a film. Then, when the cartridges ran out, he crumpled on the wet stones and cried for his mother. He was just nineteen.

They hanged him by the neck until he was dead.

I do not think they will hang Rose. They tried her, with Callaghan, for the murder of Menhennet. The jury disagreed and there is to be a re-trial some time in the New Year. The papers were very sentimental about her; they said she was more to be pitied than blamed. They do not know about Jasmine and it is easy to pity when you only know half of the truth.

I do not want to know what happens to her. I shall go abroad and not take any English papers. I should like to forget that she ever lived and sometimes, for a little while, I do forget her.

THE END